George McManus

JIGGS IS BACK

INTRODUCTION BY William Kennedy

COMMENT AND ANALYSIS BY Bill Blackbeard

CELTIC BOOK COMPANY: Berkeley, California, 1986

Jiggs is Back is published as the first volume in the new *Library of Irish American Literature and Culture*. Special thanks to Dennis Gallagher (Design), Donna DeCesare and the San Francisco Academy of Comic Art (Research), Gary Schaffer (Color Separations and Printing), Pete Hamill and Eileen Callahan (Advice and Inspiration). This book has been conceived and edited by Bob Callahan. *Jiggs is Back* is available to the retail book trade from the Subterranean Book Company, P.O. Box 10233, Eugene, Oregon 97440. The title is also available to comic bookstores everywhere through Eclipse Books, P.O. Box 199, Guerneville, California 95446.

This book is dedicated to that budding, thirteen year-old comic strip artist, David Orion Callahan.

ISBN 0-913666-82-3

Address all additional inquiries to:
CELTIC BOOK COMPANY
P.O. Box 59[illegible]5
Berkeley, California 94705

AN' HOW YOU USED TO PLAY TO ENTER-
TAIN THE BUTCHER WHO USED TO COURT
YOUR AUNT MARY- IF HE COULD BE EN-
TERTAINED- REMEMBER THE NIGHT HIS
CELLULOID COLLAR EXPLODED ?
12-22
AN' WHEN YOU WUZ A LITTLE KID-HOW
JEALOUS YOU WUZ WHEN I USED TO
TAKE MINNIE,THE TOM BOY, TO THE
BALL GAME-

AND HOW YOU AND MARY
MAHATERTY USED TO
DANCE ON THE STREET-
LATER SHE MARRIED A
COOK ON A CANAL BOAT
AND WENT TO SEA-

AND HOW TH' KILLIGANS USED TO
WATCH FOR THEIR SON "BRICK TOP"
TO COME HOME WITH HIS PAY ON
SATURDAY NIGHT- BUT SOMETIMES
HE WOULDN'T SHOW UP UNTIL
SUNDAY- AN' YOU'D HARDLY
RECOGNIZE
HIM-
12-24

AN' YOUR COUSIN "MIKE"
COMPLAINED HE COULDN'T
SLEEP NIGHTS- NO WONDER-
HE WUZ UNCONSCIOUS
ALL DAY-

AND LITTLE TESSIE KRAUTINPOT USED
TO TAKE HER DADDY'S DINNERPAIL TO
HIM EVERY DAY AT THE PICKLE WORKS-
HE LIKED FISH FOR HIS LUNCH- EVERY
CAT IN TOWN KNEW IT AND SO DID THE
NEIGHBORS-

What's the matter with Papa? I saw him drink water.

AN INTRODUCTION BY William Kennedy

JIGGS. WHEN I WAS growing up, reading him every day and especially in color on Sunday, he didn't seem any more Irish than half a dozen of our neighbors who looked like him. He seemed to me just another American victim of success, trapped by his money and his wife Maggie's social climbing in a world he loathed. He preferred old friends at the saloon, or at the construction job (Jiggs carried a hod before he got rich). Maggie chastised such recidivism by throwing rolling pins at his head.

I eventually came to realize that both Jiggs and my neighbors were indeed Irish-Americans, and that Jiggs spoke for his look-alikes in their ascendancy out of poverty into the sweet-smelling region of money. It was the specifics of these contrasting worlds that made the story of Maggie and Jiggs valuable originally and keeps it valuable today as peerless social history. Reencountering Jiggs in this book is like shedding four decades, or six. It returns us to the time when the quartet sang at Rooney's saloon until the boiler factory next door complained about the noise.

In his prime Jiggs had 80 million readers in 46 countries and 16 languages. His creator, George McManus, bragged he was as rich as Jiggs: he made $12 million in the 40 years he drew the strip. Oliver St. John Gogarty, the Irish writer, told McManus he was a genius, and Gogarty was right. Nobody invents like McManus any more. He once spent two weeks drawing one picture for the strip—a single panel of Times Square, drawn for the Sunday pages on New Year's Eve, 1939. Compared to what today passes for cartooning, Jiggs qualifies as a kind of *War and Peace* of the Golden Age of the funny papers. Charlie Chaplin said he studied Jiggs with profit, and what comic couldn't? It was heroically funny work; Jiggs, for instance, reminiscing to Maggie about her family: "Your grandpap . . . lived to be eighty and never used glasses. He drank out of the bottle . . . Your uncle Bimmy lived in the kitchen so he wouldn't have to go so far to eat."

"I was just thinking," says Maggie, "how marvelous it

is that all my relations are talented in the world of music."

"Yes," says Jiggs, "it is marvelous that you think so."

McManus probably heard such lines in the same way I did—uttered by Irishmen about Irishmen, self-criticism being a cherished Irish heritage second only to criticism of others.

There is grand hyperbole in the world of Jiggs, but it also cuts close to the real bone: realism in the funhouse, which is the foundation for so many of the major comic strips that were. To be sure some were born in cuckooland: *Popeye* and *Li'l Abner* and the *Katzenjammer Kids*, and there were the improbable worlds of *Mandrake the Magician* and *Buck Rogers*.

But think of that realism: a world hostile to children in *Little Orphan Annie* and *Little Annie Rooney*; trendy adolescence at the soda fountain in *Harold Teen*; the boxing world in *Joe Palooka*; adventure in exotic Asia and Africa in *Terry and the Pirates* and *Tim Tyler's Luck*; and then the mainstay—the family—in *Mickey Finn* and *Moon Mullins* and *Gasoline Alley* and *Blondie* . . . and *Jiggs*.

The funnies taught us about all those sweet truths that would become the essence of Hollywood's happy-ending movies. There was no divorce in the funny sheets, and no death. Life was wacko and it went on forever. Jiggs went on until 1954 when George McManus died. McManus had kept up with life, evolving the strip to conform to changing times. When the rolling pin went out of style Maggie threw vases instead. I don't remember the demise of Jiggs as a strip. Maybe my attention wandered, or more likely because the funnies went minimal, editors double-shrinking them to save space, treating them like poor relations which, predictably with such treatment, most of them became. *Pogo*, a latter-day wonder, is gone. *Beetle Bailey* endures, and so does *B.C.* and the remarkable *Peanuts*; and now Gary Trudeau with *Doonesbury* and Berke Breathed with *Bloom County* are keeping the art form respectably savage and original and funny.

But it's just not like it was and it probably won't be, either. We've climbed out of the saloon era, the soda fountain era and today Little Annie Rooney would have to be a hooker. The great comics of yore exist only as artifacts of an ebullient past. When you enter into that past in the book that follows you will, among other excursions, go on vacation across the country with Maggie and Jiggs. And when it's over you'll return to the old train station in the neighborhood where Jiggs began and you'll see the neighbors turning out to welcome the old gent.

George McManus and Charlie Chaplin on the set of "The Kid"

"My he looks grand," says one neighbor. "He's not staggerin' a bit either."

Not a bit. He stands up to time.

Welcome back, Jiggs. And stick around. We got some on ice.

OH-YA-AS, WE HUGGINS ARE LITERALLY STEEPED IN OUR FAMILY TRADITIONS - MY DEAR MRS. JIGGS - NOW HERE IS OUR GREAT-GREAT-GREAT GREAT-GRAND-UNCLE - SIR HOWE DARYOU - HE OWNED 8000 SQUARE MILES WHERE UTICA NOW STANDS AND SO IT GOES - MY DEAR -
ALL HUGGINS FAMILY HEIRLOOMS, MY DEAR FELLOW - WE BULGE WITH ANCESTRY -
AN' THEY ALL HAD PLENTY OF IRON IN THEIR BLOOD BY THE LOOKS OF IT -
WELL - GOOD-BYE AGAIN - CHAWMED BEYOND WORDS WITH YOUR VISIT - I SHALL BE DELIGHTED TO TAKE A PEEK AT SOME OF YOUR FAMILY ANTIQUES -
YOU MUST CALL AGAIN - ANY TIME - I'M IN EVERY EVENING -
CAN'T GIT OUT, EH? NEITHER CAN I -
YOU HEARD ME - YOU'RE THE ONLY ANTIQUE IN THE FAMILY NOW - BUT WE GOT TO BUILD-UP A FAMILY BACKGROUND
WELL, YOUR UNCLE OUGHT TO KNOW A LOT ABOUT GROUND, HE'S BEEN DIGGIN' IN IT FOR YEARS -
I JUST KNOW THAT THERE'S ROYAL BLOOD IN OUR FAMILY AND I WANT YOU TO HAVE IT TRACED,
WELL, HERE'S A BOOK ON ANCESTRY - BUT IT DOES-N'T SAY ANY-THING ABOUT TH' O'FINNIGANS,
THAT WILL REQUIRE SOME RESEARCH -
WELL, I'LL SEE WHAT CAN BE DONE MAGGIE'S TALKING OF A COAT OF ARMS - BY GOLLY, HER DADDY DIDN'T HAVE A COAT ON HIS BACK -
WILL TRACEM
PROFESSOR OF RESEARCH IN FAMILY TREES
ANCESTRY
CLANS
RACES
ETC -
WELL, THIS LOOKS LIKE THE MAN I WANT -
MR. TRACEM, YOU'RE HIRED, MAKE A GOOD JOB OF IT - I'VE TOLD YOU ALL ABOUT THE FAMILY - THAT IS - EXCEPT WHAT TH' POLICE WANT TO KNOW.
THANK YOU, MR. JIGGS - I SHALL START ON YOUR RESEARCH IMMEDIATELY. AND DEPEND ON IT - I'LL NOT LEAVE A BRICK UNTURNED -
ONE MONTH LATER
WHAT'S THAT? EVERYTHING IS COMPLETE? ALL RIGHT, MR TRACEM, BRING ALL OF THE DATA AND HEIRLOOMS RIGHT UP TO TH' HOUSE -
WELL, STEP INTO THE LIBRARY - ALL IS READY -
MY HEART IS ALL AFLUTTER I JUST KNOW THERE IS A KNIGHT ON MY SIDE OF THE FAMILY -
LET'S GO IN AND SEE, MOTHER -
EEK!
POP ULARRITY WANTED IN EVERY STATE BY THE POLICE
TIMOTHY'S DINNER-PAIL ALSO USED FOR BEER -
UNCLE JERRY'S BRIEF CASE 1874
ED NOT WANTED ANY-WHERE
AUNTIE BRIDGET'S COAXER
UNCLE PADDY'S FIRST SOCIAL CONNECTION
A SPADE'S A SPADE WITH
CORNED BEEF
CABBAGE
THE PICK OF THE FAMILY 1860
GRANPA DINNY'S CALLING CARDS
COUSIN LARRY'S FAMILY ROADSTER 1830
BOX MADE BY MICKEY BEFORE HE WAS HANGED
2-23

Reading the riot act, or, Sunday mornings with Maggie and Jiggs

COMMENT AND ANALYSIS BY Bill Blackbeard

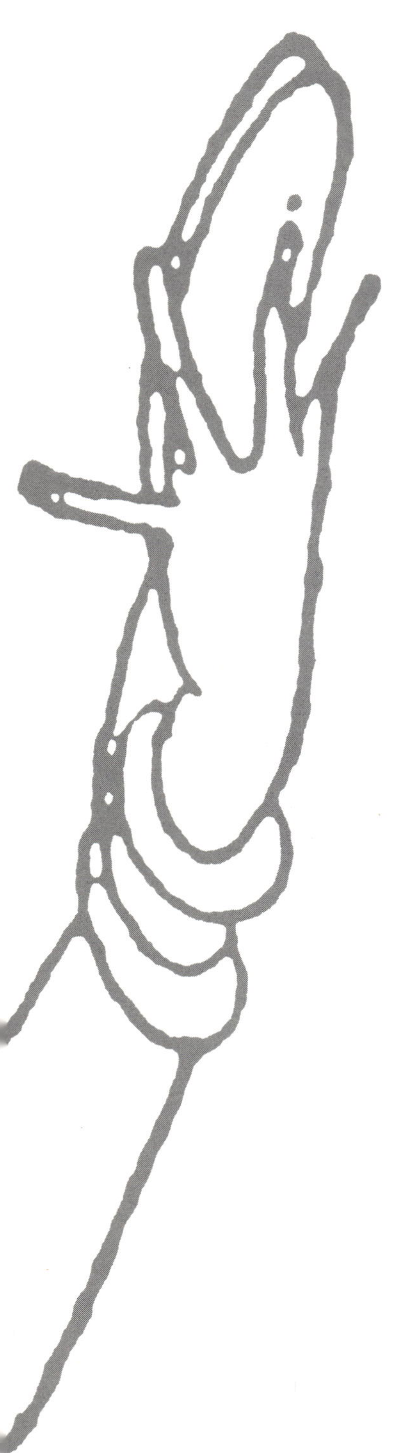

FOR THIRTY-FIVE YEARS between 1918 and 1954, George McManus's factitious Maggie and Jiggs held court from Sheboygan to San Diego as America's front-page family of the comics. Much as national newsstands now blossom in full color every Sunday morning with *Blondie* and *Peanuts* cutting up the weekend papers they engagingly enfold, so did those of the mid-century unfurl the red, white, and blue of McManus's embattled ménage: white for shattering crockery, red for the galaxies of stars circling the buffeted head of Mr. Jiggs, and blue for the air encompassing the commentaries of Mrs. Maggie as she skimmed unerring dishes at her offending spouse.

In those emblazoned years the Jiggs household also included such occasional walk-ons as their ice-maiden daughter, Nora; a seldom-seen son who spent his life flunking college; and—for a time—a spiffy new English son-in-law, Lord Worthnotten. On every Sunday front page, however, from the close of the First World War, to a decade past the end of the Second, it was the endless war of Maggie and Jiggs which served as the constant focus and point of this massively followed and devoured American classic.

In those years between the wars, with a readership still undistracted by the mind-bleeding twinkle of television, a Sunday comics front-pager reflected solid national popularity—a genuine guarantee that millions relished the showcased strip. A comic holding such a coveted spot for a succession of decades had clearly become a national institution. For an enormous number of 1920's and 1930's citizens—weighing, as they did, the comparative appeal of one newspaper's weekend armload of headlines, political punditry, and abundant magazine, movie and sports sections, over those of another—the familiar, satisfaction-assured presence of Maggie and Jiggs topside would clinch the choice every week. For millions, Maggie and Jiggs were the undisputed king and queen of the comics.

It was hard during those years for most American homes to miss the regular presence or cherished memories of the domestic imbroglios of Mr. and Mrs. Jiggs—and indeed, there were few that would have wanted to. Yet this seemingly deep-rooted epic of American folklore was unable to survive the death of George McManus in 1954, despite the attempted retention of the striking graphic style he first developed.

In sad point of fact, marked graphic mastery—or even simple competence—has rarely been a significant criterion for comic

strip success. Imaginative and effective graphic work may be present in a highly popular strip, as it was in the case of this McManus classic, or it may be virtually absent, as in other hit strips; yet, in and of itself, it is largely irrelevant to the general reader. What usually shapes wide public response to a comic strip—then, as now—is its direct relevance to what the public already knows, what it experiences almost daily. The more a strip plays with "the warp and woof of fancy," as *Krazy Kat*'s George Herriman put it, the more it risks alienating the general reader (as did critically-hailed works such as *Krazy Kat* itself—kept in print only through the direct efforts of newspaper and syndicate owner William Randolph Hearst). In McManus's time, certainly, it was those comic strips which dealt with familiar situations—family drama, well-known urban or rural stereotype caricatures, or—in the 1930's—violence and sex in easily followed formats borrowed from detective fiction or movie science-fiction modes—that caught the prompt and faithful attention of myriad readers.

But then, George McManus certainly did not know he was firming up one of the classic comic strips of all time when he set pen to paper to draw the initial Maggie and Jiggs episodes. In fact, McManus thought he had already achieved that success with his widely printed Sunday page, *Their Only Child*, when he began toying with ideas for a new and separate daily strip back in 1913. A great deal of his earlier work had been adapted on stage and screen between 1904 and 1913—notably *Panhandle Pete* and *The Newlyweds*. By then McManus was already in print in dozens of papers nationally. Both *Panhandle Pete* and *The Newlyweds* had been created, like so many other early comics, as trial balloons. Their suc-

cess had had considerably less to do with McManus's strikingly individual graphics, and far more to do with the disarming appeal of the personalities of their main protagonists.

Style helped, of course; after all, McManus *drew* funny. More to the point, he drew *familiarly* as well. People saw people they already knew in his work; and they talked to their friends about it. Such talk soon drew attention, and the circulation of the papers began to grow as well. McManus's characters became everyone's friends. People were reluctant to let them go. When McManus left the syndicate distributing *The Newlyweds* to work for William Randolph Hearst, millions of readers continued to embrace his old strip as drawn now by a gifted mimic named Carmichael. Only an even bigger hit—such as the artist was about to concoct in Maggie and Jiggs—could have persuaded his loyal public to eventually forget the preceding successes.

What snared the reader's new delight in McManus's first tentative toying with Maggie and Jiggs was the simplistic, but sharply witting reworking of a popular comic platitude of the time—the melodrama of unending domestic conflict as brought about by a presumably "inherent" feminine inclination towards culture in open warfare against a presumably "inherent" masculine inclination to avoid such concerns by escaping into business, or other various "low-brow" forms of socializing and male-bonding—the back-alley bars, and the burlesque shows—then at the height of their popularity in this country.

The genius of McManus's handling of this trussed turkey of a theme lay in the provocative switches he played in developing this platitude into a new comic form. The son of Irish immigrants—

his mother from County Limerick, his father from Westmeath—McManus was sharply aware of a new immigrant America in which—in certain, increasingly common instances—many of the new arrivals found themselves happily, and often quite suddenly, very much in the pink. McManus's Jiggs thus became a new hod-carrying type, who—by dint of some forever unexplained business acumen, and not a small amount of suggested political pull down at City Hall—had grown rather snappingly rich. On the other hand, McManus's Maggie—a former laundress—now spent her time in avid cultivation of the opera, the ballet, and not a few members of the foreign aristocratic class.

It was a wonderful, relatively new, comic scenario; and McManus played it for all that it was worth.

Rather than having Jiggs emulate other self-made men, lost now in the companionship of mere business associates in endless rounds of golf at the most exclusive country clubs, McManus preferred to establish his own parable on assimilation by sending Jiggs back to rejoin his former cronies at the construction sites, and corner saloons of his birth. This fate, needless to say, simply horrified Maggie who, quite clearly, wanted nothing whatsoever to do with her previous neighbors—either her former laundress friends, or their always grimy low-life husbands.

By depicting Maggie and Jiggs in this manner, McManus in fact universalized his characters. Jiggs's old working-class neighbors could both relish his dilemma, and appreciate his loyalty to the virtues of tavern life; while readers who had already risen to the middle-class (and higher) often still possessed parents who were working class, and proud of it. Blue-collar workers were thus reading about themselves in Jiggs's daily escapades (which reached the Sunday papers, finally, in 1918), while white-collar families just then making it to their first car and suburban home were frankly delighted in seeing their own parents—or, at the very least, their own favourite aunts and uncles—in the form of McManus's most famous characters.

There was a shared recognition—and sympathy—for Jiggs, of course; but beyond that, in her ongoing attempt to "bring Jiggs up" to the established standards of propriety and etiquette, there was no little sympathy for the character of Maggie, either. While readers could not exactly identify *with* Maggie, they could nonetheless find an essential core of truth in her mission, and enjoy as well her not entirely unfamiliar point-of-view.

When the social scene, and the national perception of American realities changed after World War II, the long-lasting appeal of the Maggie and Jiggs characters slowly began to fade. Such figures no longer seemed familiar; or, if they did, they no longer represented characters with whom most Americans wanted to feel a direct and continuing relationship. By the middle 1950's, Jiggs—still clambering out of a high Park Avenue mansion window to board a suspended girder to lunch with buddies on an adjacent construction site—seemed as alien and exotic a being as Herriman's *Krazy Kat* had become to another public, years before.

The point had been lost.

By 1954, Jiggs's very Irishness had itself more or less disappeared from the strip. Millions of younger readers had no idea that Jiggs represented any particular nationality at all—and, they no doubt would have found that fact of no import, if pointed out to them.

When George McManus died in 1954, his life-long front-page contract with the Hearst syndicate died with him. New artists were assigned to draw the feature, but these artists soon found their own efforts reduced to a third of a page on the inside of the weekly section where, ultimately, the strip passed into newspaper oblivion. One by one, most of the hundreds of papers which had once carried the strip eventually cast it adrift.

No news item appeared to note its final passing.

The graphic glory of McManus's work has, however, remained undimmed through the ensuing years. Seen again now, these Sunday pages have as much lustre for our own eyes as they did for their original millions of readers more than sixty years ago. Selected for this book to showcase a triad of outstanding stories or themes in the Sunday strip, the episodes that follow reflect some of the more graphically imaginative departures McManus (and his able assistant of the 1930's and later, Zeke Zekely) took from more routine domestic concerns.

The first group of Sunday pages to appear in this book cover Maggie and Jiggs's return to poverty in the early 1920's. Having gone bust in the movie business—reflecting, perhaps, McManus's view of the Hollywood of the time—Jiggs is faced with the very kind of hand-to-mouth existence from which he had climbed only a decade or so earlier. Needless to say, the thematic exigencies of the strip made this narrative jape a brief one. Maggie and Jiggs, it may be reported, found themselves back in the chips within a matter of weeks.

Instigated by the unexpected marriage of daughter Nora to an

ROSIE-DARLING-ISN'T IT NICE TO BE ALONE ? JUST YOU AND I- ISN'T THE WORLD WONDERFUL ?
I'M SO HAPPY-
THAT MAN AGAIN-
HOW DID YOU GET IN HERE ?
I JUST CAN'T REMEMBER- BUT I WOULD LIKE TO KNOW HOW TO GET OUT- DO YOU MIND ?
AS LONG AS I DON'T BELONG UP HERE- I MIGHT AS WELL GET OUT OF THE PICTURE-- TOODLE-OO-
?
STRANGE FELLOW- BUT I'M GLAD HE HAS GONE-
WHAT'S THAT-?
HORRORS- IT MUST BE THAT PECULIAR CREATURE AGAIN--
4-17
CRASH!
BANG!
WHAT'S THIS ?
OH- WE ARE GLAD YOU DROPPED IN- SIR VON PLATTER-
I'M SORRY IF I'M INTRUDING- BUT I HAVE AN ENGAGEMENT SOMEWHERE THIS EVENING- I MUST HAVE OR I WOULDN'T BE DRESSED UP LIKE THIS-- DO YOU MIND IF I 'PHONE MY HOUSE ?
WHAT ARE YOU GONNA DO? CALL YOURSELF UP?
GREAT HEAVENS- I THINK HE HAS FALLEN DOWN-STAIRS-
HE PROBABLY FELL UPSTAIRS- HE NEVER DOES ANYTHING LIKE ANYONE ELSE-
?
WHAT IN THE WORLD ARE YOU TRYING TO DO? COME BACK IN THE PICTURE-
CAREFUL- DO NOT BUMP HIS HEAD-
THAT'S WHAT'S TH' MATTER WITH HIM- I THINK HE'S BEEN BUMPED ON THE HEAD YEARS AGO-
COME TO THINK OF IT- IT IS NO USE CALLING MY HOME AS I HAVE NO 'PHONE- AND BESIDES- I AM THE ONLY ONE THERE--
WELL- DO TRY AND THINK WHERE YOU ARE TO GO- SOMEBODY WILL BE TERRIBLY DISAPPOINTED IF YOU DON'T SHOW UP-
LEAVE HIM ALONE- HE'S LIABLE TO THINK ANY MINUTE-- I WONDER WHETHER HE KIN TELL WHEN HE'S UNCONSCIOUS
THINK- NOW TRY HARD-
I KNOW I'M NOT GOING TO THE OPERA AS I WAS AT THE THEATRE AND IT IS CLOSED--AND I KNOW I HAVEN'T AN ENGAGEMENT WITH MY AUNT- AS I HAVE NO AUNT-
I FORGOT- DO YOU MIND ?
AH- THERE YOU ARE- SIR VON PLATTER- I AM SURPRISED THAT YOU REMEMBERED TO TAKE ME TO THE BIG SCHOOL DANCE TONIGHT-
OH- DID HE HAVE THE DATE WITH YOU ?
THAT'S RIGHT- ISN'T IT LUCKY YOU ARE HERE? I'D NEVER HAVE FOUND YOU-
NOW- JUST SIT RIGHT THERE- I MUST RUN UPSTAIRS AND HELP MY DAUGHTER GET HER WRAPS ON-
DO YOU MIND IF I GO INTO THE LIBRARY? AND PLEASE REMEMBER I AM IN THERE AS I MIGHT FORGET-
NOW- WHERE IN THE WORLD IS THAT FOOL?
4-17
WELL- I CAN'T FIND HIM- HE SAID HE WAS GOING IN THE LIBRARY-
WELL- I'LL NOT WAIT FOR HIM- I'LL CALL UP THAT GOOD-LOOKING BILL GOODFRIEND- TO TAKE ME-
THAT GUY'S FOLKS MUST HAVE BEEN VERY FOND OF KIDS TO RAISE HIM-
THIS ISN'T A LIBRARY- NOW HOW DID I GET OUT HERE ?? WHERE AM I ?
GEO McMANUS

I PROMISED ROSIE THAT I'D CALL HER AT THIS TIME - I HOPE THE BOSS ISN'T IN SO I CAN USE HIS 'PHONE -
OH! I BEG YOUR PARDON, BOSS -
JUST A MINUTE, ARCHIE, I WANT TO TALK TO YOU JUST AS SOON AS I FINISH 'PHONING -
WHAT'LL I DO NOW?
I'D SUGGEST TURNING IT AROUND BUT I THINK IT'S A LITTLE LATE -
WHAT IN THE WORLD HAS HAPPENED TO ARCHIE? HE'S JUST FORGOTTEN TO PHONE - HE JUST FORGETS ABOUT ME, I'LL NEVER SPEAK TO HIM ANY MORE -
ONE HOUR LATER, AND STILL ON THE 'PHONE
YES, I DECIDED TO BUY YOUR GOODS BUT MAKE ME A BETTER PRICE -
GOSH, WHAT WILL ROSIE THINK OF ME NOW - ?
DEAR, GET UP - COUNT DE FECTIVE IS HERE TO SEE YOU, AND HE HAS A FRIEND OF YOURS WITH HIM -
THE FRIEND IS DINTY MOORE - AS MR. MOORE IS A FRIEND OF THE COUNT'S, I HAVEN'T ANY OBJECTION TO DINTY -
WELL, MAGGIE YOU GLADDEN ME HEART WITH THEM WORDS -
WELL, DINTY, THIS IS A SURPRISE TO SEE YOU IN ME HOUSE
YES, AN' IT'S SOMETHIN' NEW FOR YOU TO GIT IN YER PARLOR, ISN'T IT?
MR. MOORE HAS ENGAGED ME TO BE HIS SOCIAL ADVISER, AND I'VE HIRED HIM TO ACQUAINT ME WITH YOUR COUNTRY -
AN' I'VE DECIDED TO GIVE A BEEFSTEAK PARTY TO THE GANG AND I WANT YOU ON TH' COMMITTEE, IF YOUR WIFE DON'T OBJECT -
YOU JUST TELL MRS. JIGGS THAT I THINK IT'S A GRAND IDEA -
ALL RIGHT - BUT IF I DON'T COME BACK - COME AN' GIT ME -
WHY, CERTAINLY, WHAT-EVER THE COUNT SAYS IS ALWAYS ALL-RIGHT I'M SO GLAD TO SEE YOU INTERESTED IN THE ROYALTY -
MAGGIE - ME DARLIN' - AT LAST WE'RE BEGINNING TO UNDERSTAND EACH OTHER -
I'LL 'PHONE DUGAN, CASEY, MORAN AN' GROGAN, O'BRIEN AN' MC MAHON - THEY SHOULD BE ON THE COMMITTEE TOO - THEY ARE GOOD FIGHTERS -
TELL 'EM TO COME HERE RIGHT AWAY AN' BRING SOME OF THE GANG -
JOLLY!
WE 'PHONED FOR SOME OF TH' BOYS TO COME UP, MAGGIE -
IS IT O.K., MRS. JIGGS?
CALL ME MAGGIE, DINTY, SURE, IT'S ALL RIGHT - I'LL BE GLAD TO SING THE OLD SONGS FOR THEM -
IS IT REALLY SAFE TO COME IN, OR IS IT JUST A TRICK - ?
HELLO - BOYS - STEP RIGHT IN -
HOWDY, GANG - STEP RIGHT THIS WAY -
COME IN, BOYS, AN' FERGIT YOUR MANNERS
THIS IS GOING TO BE A JOLLY PARTY
BY GOLLY - THIS REMINDS ME OF TH' DAYS IN TH' GOOD OL' NEIGHBORHOOD
TH' OLD LADY IS LIKE SHE WUZ IN THE OLD DAYS -
LITTLE ANNIE ROONEY IS MY SWEET-HEART -
COUNT - GIT ME ANOTHER GLASS OF BEER -
GET UP - DO YOU THINK YOU'RE GOIN' TO SLEEP ALL DAY - ?
IF I COULD DREAM LIKE THAT - I'D NEVER WANT TO WAKE UP.
DADDY, I WANT MY ALLOWANCE - I'M GOIN' SHOPPIN'
GEO MC MANUS
2-2

English aristocrat, Lord Worthnotten, we next pursue a full national tour with the entire Jiggs ménage. Since Maggie felt the new son-in-law should have a good look at the country he had married into, a prolonged trip to many of the major cities was undertaken, a trip spread over the better part of a year in both the daily and Sunday strips. Incorporating the scenic attributes of such locales as Los Angeles, Chicago, Washington D.C., and Manhattan provoked one of the finest concentrations of graphic fancy to appear in the long run of the McManus classic (and it also allowed McManus to tip his fedora to avid readers in those locales which the strip visited and depicted).

And finally, in the closing segment, we find Maggie and Jiggs in an uncharacteristically quieter moment reflecting upon their own, increasingly distant, Irish American urban past. These pages ran primarily in the 1930's and early 1940's, and were always greeted by real McManus fans with a special relish each time they appeared. The great majority of these pages have been assembled here in the original sequential order, and are liable to prove the real high point of this book for readers with an interest in the color and variety of American social history. The scenes and types recalled are at once marvellously accurate, as well as graphically and exquisitely funny to look at. These pages take us back to an ancestral America we may never have seen realized so sharply, or so memorably before.

In parting, the comic intensity and execution of the nonsequential Sunday pages which have been included with this essay seemed so remarkable that they simply demanded the space that has been given to them. The Sunday-page "topper" strip, on the other hand, was added to the full-page of the early 1920's when the Hearst syndicate decided to cut their Sunday-page comics into unequal halves—thus making it possible for subscribing newspapers to tell their readers they would now be receiving twice as many "funnies" as before in the very same space! This feature has been retained in the present book both to provide proper page-balance—as well as for the extra amusement it affords.

But school is out; I have distracted you long enough. Join Jiggs and Maggie now in the comic world of half a century ago for what clearly should be a reading of sheer and marvelous delight.

The joys of poverty

SO WE'RE BROKE NOW. ALL ON ACCOUNT OF YOUR GOING INTO THE MOVIE BUSINESS IT'S TERRIBLE!

YEP I'M BUSTED WELL HAVE TO GIT A CHEAP PLACE TO LIVE AN I'LL HAVE TO GO TO WORK!

I'M THE DEPUTY SHERIFF AND I'VE TAKEN POSSESSION OF THIS HOUSE YOU'LL HAVE TO BEAT IT

I KNEW YOU'D BE ON TIME

I'LL BE BRAVE BUT IT IS VERY HARD ON ME!

I'M READY TO GO!

SHUT UP THIS IS MY PRIVATE PROPERTY AND I'M GOING TO KEEP IT COME HERE AND HELP ME INSTEAD OF STANDING THERE LIKE A DUMMY-

DO YOU EXPECT ME TO CARRY THAT?

OH! MOTHER-LEAVE THE OLD PIANO BEHIND!

I WILL NOT!

THERE'S CLANCY- HEY-GIVE US A HAUL WILL YE? I'M BROKE NOW-

YOU KNOW I WILL JIGGS!

WHERE ARE WE GOING?

DID YOU GET A PLACE?

I DID! I'VE TAKEN A LITTLE SHACK OUT IN THE COUNTRY-GO RIGHT OUT THE MAIN ROAD CLANCY!

I'LL DRIVE SLOW SO THE FAMILY KIN FOLLOW!

ISN'T THIS LOVELY- I'M HAPPY AGAIN OUT HERE IN THE COUNTRY

DON'T WORRY- MAGGIE- WE'LL GIT ALONG!

YOU'LL NEVER BE IN WANT AS LONG AS JIGGS HAS A PICK!

HAVE SOME MORE CORNED BEEF-CLANCY- YOU DON'T EAT LIKE YOU DID IN THE OLDEN DAYS!

THIS IS THE FIRST CHANCE I'VE HAD IN A LONG TIME!

I'M GOING TO SING FOR YOU BOYS IN A MINUTE!

EVERYTHING WUZ FINE UP TO NOW!

DOWN BY THE BABBLING BROOK!

THERE'S A LOT OF WORSE THINGS THAN BEIN' POOR!

IT'S TOO BAD THAT THE SHERIFF DIDN'T TAKE HER VOICE-

MAGGIE-I KNOW YOU ARE TIRED OUT GO TO BED CLANCY AN' I WILL DO THE DISHES!

YOU ARE SO THOUGHTFUL

WELL-I MUST BE GITTIN' ON ME WAY!

JUST A MINUTE-CLANCY I HAVE ONE MORE FAVOR TO ASK YOU-

WHAT'LL I DO WITH IT-JIGGS?

PAWN IT!

GEO McMANUS

BY GOLLY - YOU HAVE TO BE POOR TO BE HAPPY!
SOAP

HOW DO YOU EXPECT ME TO COOK WHEN WE HAVE NO COAL?
MOTHER - PLEASE DON'T QUARREL WITH DADDY -
I DON'T KNOW HOW I'M GONNA GIT ANY BUT I'LL TRY!
1
CASSIDY - HOW D'YE GIT COAL AROUND HERE?
WELL - JIGGS - I'VE BEEN TRYIN' FER TEN YEARS AN' THE ONLY WAY I KNOW IS TO BUY IT!
2
A SCUTTLE LIKE THAT FILLED WILL COST A DOLLAR!
COAL OFFICE
I SAID COAL - NOT GOLD!
HAY AND FEE
FOR SALE
3
I'M IN LUCK - IT'S LEAKIN'!
K.LI
COA
4
BY GOLLY - I WISH I HAD BROUGHT THE BATH - TUB!
K.LINKER
COAL CO
5
6
I WONDER IF I'M IN THE SAME CITY?
7
NOW I'M AFRAID TO GO HOME BECAUSE I LOST THE COAL BUCKET!
8
IF THIS SCHEME OF MINE WORKS - I'LL HAVE COAL TO BURN!
9
YOU BIG FAT - HEADS WHO TOLD YOU THAT YOU COULD RUN A LOCOMOTIVE?
71144
D.T.R.R.
10
IT WORKED!
D.T.R.R.
© 1923 BY INT'L FEATURE SERVICE, INC.
GREAT BRITAIN RIGHTS RESERVED
11
HERE YOU ARE - MAGGIE!
YOU DARLING!
GEO McMANUS
12

BY GOLLY! YE CAN'T BUY HAPPINESS- YOU GOTTA BE POOR TO GIT IT!

WHAT IN THE WORLD ARE WE GOING TO DO? THERE'S NO FOOD OR COAL IN THE HOUSE I SEE NOTHING IN SIGHT BUT THE POOR-HOUSE!
I SUPPOSE I'LL HAVE TO GO OUT AN' LOOK FOR WORK!
1

YOU'RE A DARLING I KNOW YOU'LL FIND SOMETHING TO DO!
THAT'S WHAT I'M AFRAID OF!
2

IF YOU PASS CASEY'S BRICK YARD ASK PADDY DUGAN AND HIS WIFE TO COME OVER TODAY.
BY GOLLY- IT SOUNDS LIKE THE GOOD OLD DAYS!
3

THAT'S A FINE SIGN-
WASHING AND IRONING DONE HERE
4

AN' MAGGIE'S A CHAMPION AT A TUB!
WASHING AND IRONING DONE HERE
5

THIS WILL BRING IN SOME BUSINESS!
WASHING AND IRONING DONE HERE
6

HELLO-MRS. JIGGS- I HAVE SOME WASHIN' TO BE DONE- ARE YOU DOIN THE WORK?
I HAVEN'T DONE ANY IN YEARS BUT I'LL TRY!
7

I HAVE SOME WASHIN' HERE
WHEN CAN YOU GIVE MY LAUNDRY BACK?
I HAVE SOME IRONIN' TO BE DONE!
8

YOU WASHEE COLLARS AND CUFFS?
WELL-FOR THE LOVE OF MIKE-
WHAT IS THIS ALL ABOUT- MOTHER?
9

WASHING AND IRONING DONE HERE
SO! THAT'S THE CAUSE OF ALL THIS!
TUM-TE-UM-TUM TIDDLE-DE
10

COME HERE- YOU BRUTE!
© 1923 BY INT'L FEATURE SERVICE, INC.
GREAT BRITAIN RIGHTS RESERVED
11

I'M GLAD SHE BROKE THE SIGN ON MY HEAD- OR I'D BE GITTIN' MORE OF THIS TO DO!
GEO McMANUS
12

MAGGIE - I'M GOIN' OUT AN' LOOK FER A JOB AN' I WON'T COME HOME UNTIL I GIT ONE:

BE SURE TO COME BACK IF YOU DO GET ONE:

1

HELLO - DAN - ANY CHANCE OF GITTIN A JOB HERE?

THEY'RE LOOKIN' FOR A GUY HERE TO MIND THE STAGE DOOR - GO SEE THE MANAGER HE AINT GOT NO SENSE - HE MIGHT HIRE YOU!

STAGE DOOR

2

IF YOU'RE LOOKIN' FER AN INTELLIGENT MAN FOR THAT STAGE DOOR JOB YOU'RE LUCKY THAT I CAME IN

I'LL GIVE YOU A TRIAL - MY SECRETARY WILL INSTRUCT YOU IN WHAT YOU ARE TO DO:

3

BY GOLLY! THIS IS A BETTER JOB THAN I THOUGHT!

STAGE DOOR

4

SAY - YOUSE GUYS HAVE GOT TO LEND ME FIFTY DOLLARS - I GOT A JOB AN' I NEED NEW CLOTHES

YOU KNOW US OLD 'PAL'!

WHY SURE:

GIVE 'IM TEN FOR ME - DINTY - I'LL PAY YOU WHEN I WIN!

5

OH! ARE YOU THE NEW STAGE DOOR MAN?

HOW LOVELY!

THEY'RE COMMENCIN' TO SIT UP AN TAKE NOTICE ALREADY!

6

LISTEN - DINTY - I'M GONNA LEAVE MY GLAD RAGS HERE TILL TONIGHT - I'LL BE BACK TO PUT THEM ON!

THE PLACE IS YOURS - YOU KNOW THAT - JIGGS OLD BOY!

7

WELL - I'M WORKIN' IN A THEATRE MAGGIE - HURRY UP WITH THE SUPPER - I'VE GOT TO RUSH BACK - WE'RE VERY BUSY -

ISN'T THAT GRAND. SIT RIGHT DOWN AN' EAT THIS WHILE IT'S HOT!

8

HE'S A GREAT MAN - I ALWAYS DID ADMIRE THE SHAPE OF HIS HEAD - I WONDER WHAT HIS POSITION IS I'LL GET FIXED UP AN RUN DOWN TO THE THEATRE TO SEE!

9

IS THERE A MAN NAMED JIGGS WORKIN' AT THIS THEATRE

I'M THE ONLY ONE THAT DOES ANY WORK AROUND HERE YOU MIGHT INQUIRE AT THE STAGE DOOR!

10

?

WILL YOU TAKE CARE OF "WAFFLES" FOR ME UNTIL AFTER THE SHOW?

LET ME PIN THIS FLOWER ON YOU - A STAGE DOOR JOHNNY SENT ME A LOT OF 'EM!

ANY MAIL FOR ME MR. JIGGS?

STAGE DOOR

11

MR. GROGAN HAVE YOU GOT ANY KIND OF A JOB FOR THIS?

GROGAN'S COALYARD

PUT HIM DOWN - I'LL GIVE HIM A JOB:

GEO McMANUS

12

THERE IS NO COMPANY CALLING TODAY SO I COOKED YOU SOME CORNED BEEF AND CABBAGE!
I HOPE WE NEVER HAVE ANY COMPANY!
I'M GLAD TO SEE YOU SO HAPPY DADDY!

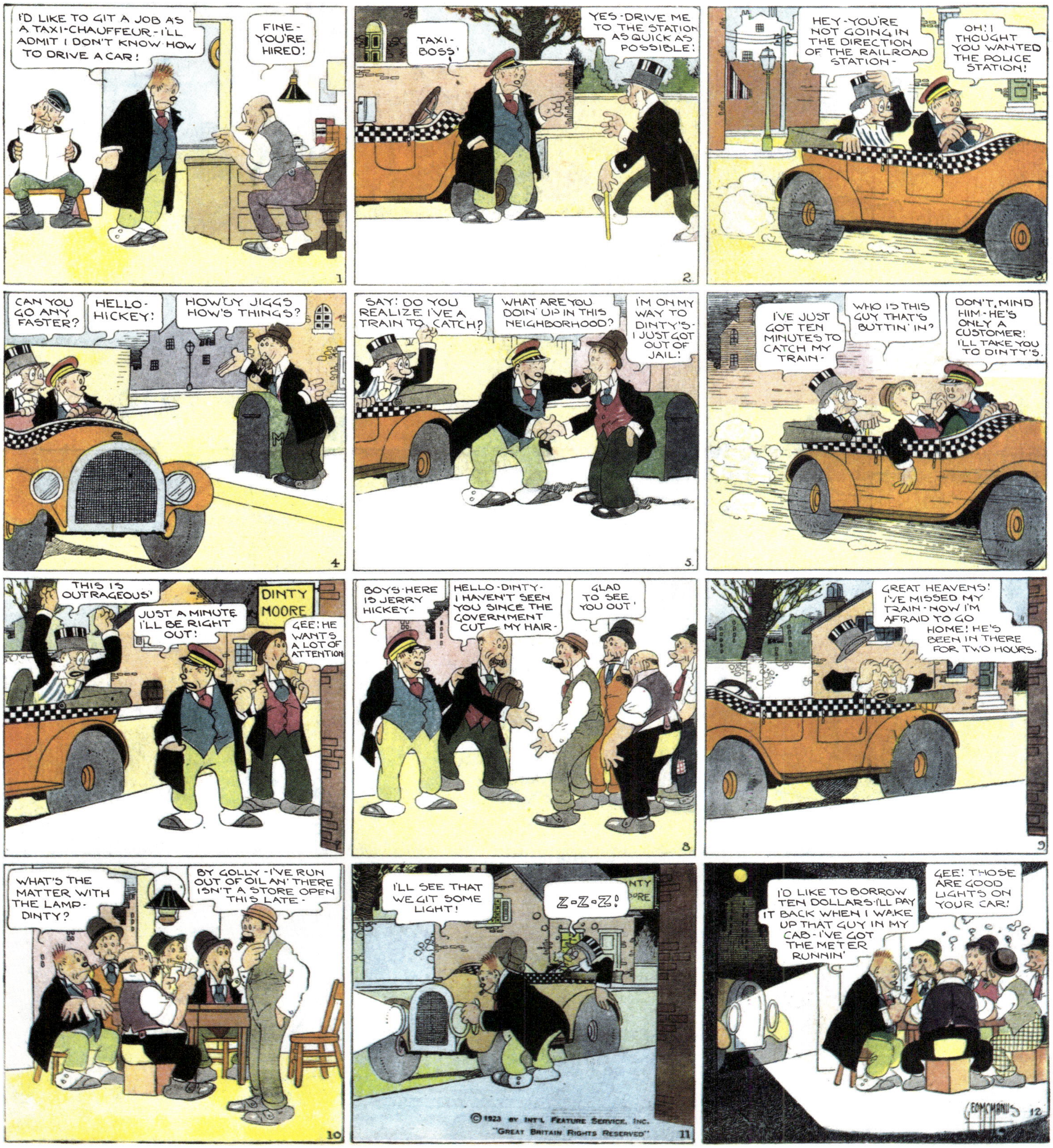

I'D LIKE TO GIT A JOB AS A TAXI-CHAUFFEUR - I'LL ADMIT I DON'T KNOW HOW TO DRIVE A CAR!
FINE - YOU'RE HIRED!
1
TAXI - BOSS!
YES - DRIVE ME TO THE STATION AS QUICK AS POSSIBLE!
2
HEY - YOU'RE NOT GOING IN THE DIRECTION OF THE RAILROAD STATION -
OH! I THOUGHT YOU WANTED THE POLICE STATION!
3
CAN YOU GO ANY FASTER?
HELLO - HICKEY!
HOW'DY JIGGS HOW'S THINGS?
4
SAY! DO YOU REALIZE I'VE A TRAIN TO CATCH?
WHAT ARE YOU DOIN' UP IN THIS NEIGHBORHOOD?
I'M ON MY WAY TO DINTY'S - I JUST GOT OUT OF JAIL!
5
I'VE JUST GOT TEN MINUTES TO CATCH MY TRAIN -
WHO IS THIS GUY THAT'S BUTTIN' IN?
DON'T MIND HIM - HE'S ONLY A CUSTOMER! I'LL TAKE YOU TO DINTY'S.
6
THIS IS OUTRAGEOUS!
JUST A MINUTE I'LL BE RIGHT OUT!
DINTY MOORE
GEE! HE WANTS A LOT OF ATTENTION
7
BOYS - HERE IS JERRY HICKEY -
HELLO - DINTY - I HAVEN'T SEEN YOU SINCE THE GOVERNMENT CUT MY HAIR -
GLAD TO SEE YOU OUT!
8
GREAT HEAVENS! I'VE MISSED MY TRAIN - NOW I'M AFRAID TO GO HOME! HE'S BEEN IN THERE FOR TWO HOURS.
9
WHAT'S THE MATTER WITH THE LAMP - DINTY?
BY GOLLY - I'VE RUN OUT OF OIL AN' THERE ISN'T A STORE OPEN THIS LATE -
10
I'LL SEE THAT WE GIT SOME LIGHT!
Z-Z-Z!
NTY
ORE
11
I'D LIKE TO BORROW TEN DOLLARS - I'LL PAY IT BACK WHEN I WAKE UP THAT GUY IN MY CAB - I'VE GOT THE METER RUNNIN'
GEE! THOSE ARE GOOD LIGHTS ON YOUR CAR!
GEO McMANUS
12

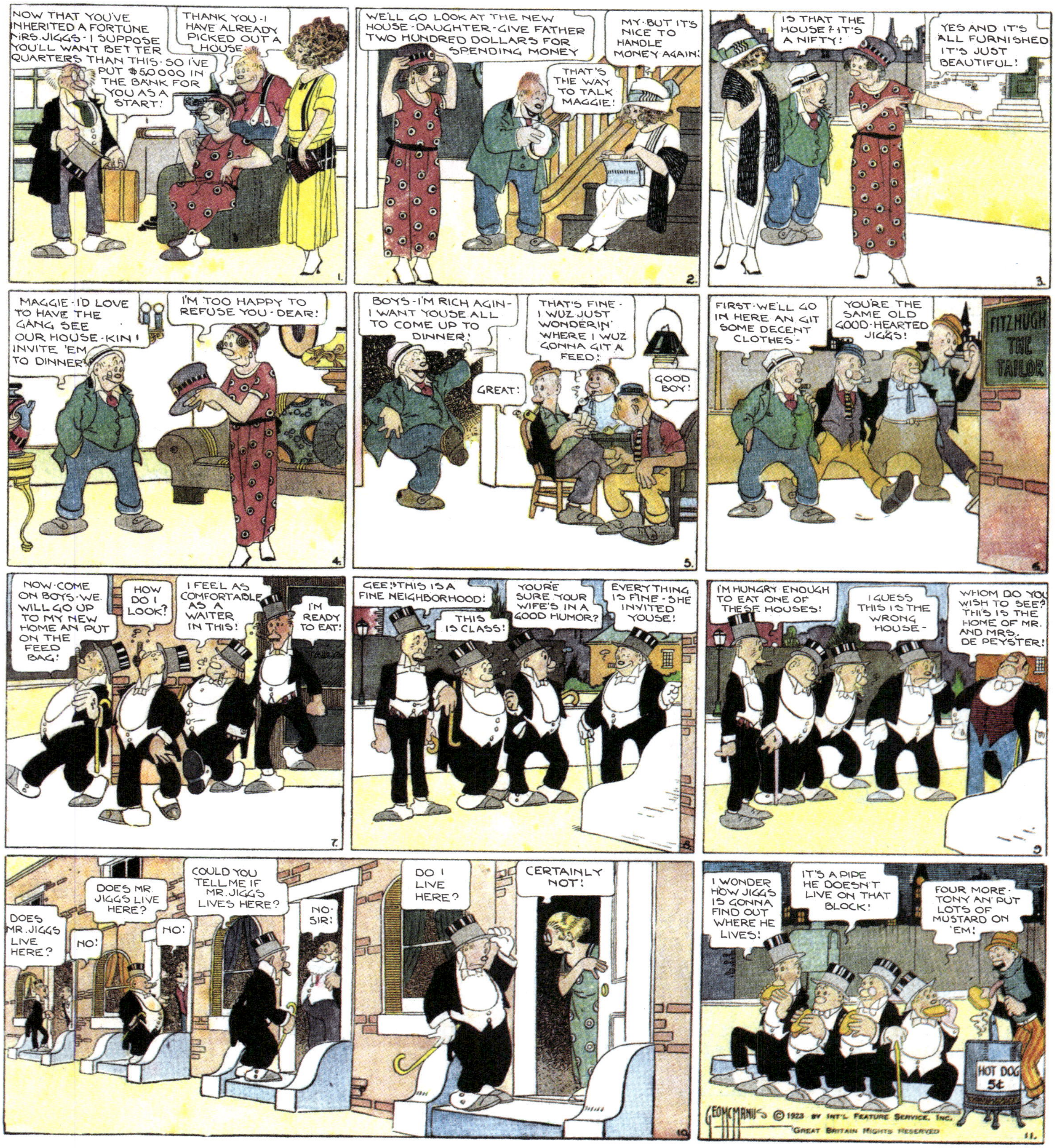

NOW THAT YOU'VE INHERITED A FORTUNE MRS. JIGGS - I SUPPOSE YOU'LL WANT BETTER QUARTERS THAN THIS - SO I'VE PUT $50,000 IN THE BANK FOR YOU AS A START!
THANK YOU - I HAVE ALREADY PICKED OUT A HOUSE.
1.

WE'LL GO LOOK AT THE NEW HOUSE - DAUGHTER - GIVE FATHER TWO HUNDRED DOLLARS FOR SPENDING MONEY
MY - BUT IT'S NICE TO HANDLE MONEY AGAIN!
THAT'S THE WAY TO TALK MAGGIE!
2.

IS THAT THE HOUSE? - IT'S A NIFTY!
YES AND IT'S ALL FURNISHED IT'S JUST BEAUTIFUL!
3.

MAGGIE - I'D LOVE TO HAVE THE GANG SEE OUR HOUSE - KIN I INVITE 'EM TO DINNER?
I'M TOO HAPPY TO REFUSE YOU - DEAR!
4.

BOYS - I'M RICH AGIN - I WANT YOUSE ALL TO COME UP TO DINNER!
THAT'S FINE - I WUZ JUST WONDERIN' WHERE I WUZ GONNA GIT A FEED!
GREAT!
GOOD BOY!
5.

FIRST - WE'LL GO IN HERE AN GIT SOME DECENT CLOTHES -
YOU'RE THE SAME OLD GOOD-HEARTED JIGGS!
FITZHUGH THE TAILOR
6.

NOW - COME ON BOYS - WE WILL GO UP TO MY NEW HOME AN PUT ON THE FEED BAG!
HOW DO I LOOK?
I FEEL AS COMFORTABLE AS A WAITER IN THIS!
I'M READY TO EAT!
7.

GEE! THIS IS A FINE NEIGHBORHOOD!
THIS IS CLASS!
YOU'RE SURE YOUR WIFE'S IN A GOOD HUMOR?
EVERYTHING IS FINE - SHE INVITED YOUSE!
8.

I'M HUNGRY ENOUGH TO EAT ONE OF THESE HOUSES!
I GUESS THIS IS THE WRONG HOUSE -
WHOM DO YOU WISH TO SEE? THIS IS THE HOME OF MR. AND MRS. DE PEYSTER!
9

DOES MR. JIGGS LIVE HERE?
NO!
DOES MR JIGGS LIVE HERE?
NO!
COULD YOU TELL ME IF MR. JIGGS LIVES HERE?
NO - SIR!
DO I LIVE HERE?
CERTAINLY NOT!
10.

I WONDER HOW JIGGS IS GONNA FIND OUT WHERE HE LIVES!
IT'S A PIPE HE DOESN'T LIVE ON THAT BLOCK!
FOUR MORE - TONY AN' PUT LOTS OF MUSTARD ON 'EM!
HOT DOG 5¢
GEO MCMANUS
11.

The vacation

ARCHIE-DON'T BE ASHAMED-TAKE ANY KIND OF A JOB-I KNOW YOU WILL SUCCEED SOME DAY-
YOU'RE RIGHT-ROSIE-I'LL HIDE MY PRIDE AN' TAKE THE FIRST JOB I CAN GET-
ROSIE IS REALLY A WONDERFUL GIRL-SHE MAKES ONE REALIZE THERE IS SOMETHING TO LIVE FOR-

HELLO-JIM-YOU LOOK SAD-WHAT'S WRONG?
WHY-THAT FATHEADED BOSS OF MINE WANTS ME TO WEAR A UNIFORM SO I QUIT ABOUT AN HOUR AGO-
Copr. 1939, King Features Syndicate, Inc., World rights reserved

?
SO LONG-JIM-
12-3

YES-ROSIE-I'VE GOT A JOB-NO-THEY DIDN'T EXACTLY SEND FOR ME-DEAR-

WELL-WE ARE GOING TO TAKE IN BOULDER DAM TODAY-MAGGIE HAS MADE ALL THE ARRANGEMENTS-
I'VE ALWAYS WANTED TO SEE THE BOULDER DAM-BY THE WAY-WHAT IS IT?

YES-NOW YOU BOYS GET YOUR HATS-WE ARE READY TO START-THE CAR AND GUIDE ARE READY-
I AM READY-
AS YOU SAY IN AMERICA-"LET'S GO"-

BOULDER DAM
FOR GOODNESS SAKE-WILL YOU LISTEN-MAGGIE?
YES-MUM-WE ARE NOW COMING TO LAKE MEAD-IT IS 227 SQUARE MILES OF WATER-THE WATER PRESSURE AT TH' BASE OF THE DAM IS 45,000 POUNDS PER SQUARE FOOT-AND THE--

REALLY?
RIGHT BELOW HERE IS THE SPILLWAY-IT HAS FOUR DRUM GATES--THE CANYON OUTLET VALVES ARE ON THE OTHER SIDE-YOU CAN SEE THE INTAKE TOWERS FROM HERE-
I WISH I HAD BOUGHT THAT HAT IN LAS VEGAS-
LOOK AT THIS AD-A COAT FOR $200-

THE RESERVOIR IS 1229 FEET ABOVE SEA LEVEL-
DEAR-ASK HIM WHICH IS THE BEST STORE IN BOULDER DAM-
AND IF THERE IS A MANICURE SHOP THERE?

NOW-HAVING TOLD YOU ABOUT THE PENSTOCKS AND THE PRESSURE TUNNELS--SHUT-OFF VALVES AND TH' COFFERDAM-WE NOW COME TO THE INLETS TO TURBINE CASINGS AND THE TOWER-CONTROLS-THE RESERVOIR OUTLETS-ETC-
THIS WOULD MAKE A SWELL BREWERY-
IT LOOKS LIKE A LADIES' HAIR-DRESSING PARLOR-
I WISH THAT GUIDE WOULD TALK ENGLISH-

GEO McMANUS
MOTHER-I THINK I SEE A LADY WITH ONE OF THOSE NEW STYLE HATS-
WHERE DO YOU THINK I CAN GET A DRINK OF WATER?
I HAVEN'T THE SLIGHTEST IDEA-
12-3

ARCHIE - I'M PROUD OF YOU - NO MATTER WHAT KIND OF A JOB YOU TAKE - I KNOW YOU WILL SUCCEED - YOU'RE DESTINED TO BE A GREAT LEADER SOME DAY -
THANKS - ROSIE DARLING - I'LL TAKE ANY KIND OF WORK - BUT YOU AND I WILL KEEP IT A SECRET -
AH - THAT'S A RELIEF - I'LL TAKE ANY KIND OF WORK - BUT I DON'T WANT ANY OF THE BOYS AT TH' OFFICE THAT WERE FIRED TO KNOW I HAVE TO STOOP TO ANY KIND OF A JOB -
YES - HERE'S THE PLACE - THEY WANT A YOUNG MAN TO RUN ERRANDS AND ALSO ACT AS BUNDLE-WRAPPER - I'LL TAKE THAT JOB -
BOY WANTED
WALK IN
BOY WANTED
OH - HELLO - FELLOWS - NICE DAY -
WALK IN
YEA - AND A NICE JOB IF I GET IT -
LOOKING FOR WORK TOO - EH - ARCHIE ?
WE GOT HERE FIRST -
SIT DOWN AND TAKE YER TURN -
12-10

WELL - HERE WE ARE IN CHICAGO - THIS IS A CITY I HAVE ALWAYS WANTED TO VISIT -
WE MUSTN'T MISS ANY OF THE SIGHTS OF INTEREST HERE IN CHICAGO -
WE'LL HAVE TO COVER A LOT OF GROUND AS OUR STAY HERE IS VERY SHORT -
WELL - I'VE GOT THIS PORTFOLIO WITH ALL THE PLACES TO SEE - I'LL LOOK IT OVER - - WHILE YOU GET THE LUGGAGE STRAIGHTENED OUT -

NOW - LET'S SEE - THEY WON'T WANT TO GO TO THE STOCK YARDS - A DRIVE THROUGH LINCOLN PARK - AND A SPIN ON LAKE SHORE DRIVE - OH - YES - WE'LL HAVE TO SEE TH' FIELD MUSEUM -

WELL - I'VE GOT ALL TH' PLACES TO SEE WRITTEN DOWN - AND I HAVE IT TIMED SO WE WILL BE ABLE TO COVER THE GROUND IN TWO DAYS -

DADDY - - IF MOTHER ASKS FOR ME - I'M GOING TO HAVE MY HAIR FIXED -
HUM - I DIDN'T COUNT ON THAT - I WILL HAVE TO LEAVE OUT A FEW PLACES -

WHERE DO YOU THINK YOU ARE GOING ?
I'M NOT THINKIN' ABOUT IT - I AM GOING - MRS. JIGGS WANTS ME TO GO TO THE STORE FOR HER -

IF WE'RE GOIN' TO SEE THIS CITY - WE HAD BETTER GIT STARTED -

DON'T DISTURB US - DEAR - WE GIRLS WILL BE QUITE BUSY FOR SOME TIME -

AH - MR. JIGGS - WON'T YOU SIT DOWN AND HAVE A SIP OF TEA ? THIS IS AN OLD BUDDY OF MINE WHO FOUND OUT I WAS IN THIS COUNTRY - JOIN US FOR A CHAT -
WELL - WHO FOUND HIM ?

CALL FOR MISTER MORAN MOORE -
BAH - I'LL WAIT IN THE LOBBY - AT LEAST I KIN WATCH THE PLANTS GROW UNTIL THEY GET READY -
Copr. 1939, King Features Syndicate, Inc., World rights reserved.

ARE YOU TO BE HERE FOR SOME TIME ?
JUST LONG ENOUGH TO SEE THE CITY -
MUTH-AW - HAVE YOU GOT MY MANICURE SET IN YOUR GRIP ?
I WONDER IF I LEFT THOSE ROAD MAPS IN THE CAR ?
I WANT SOME CANDY -
I HOPE THEY SEE MORE OF THE TOWN THAN I WILL -
GEO McMANUS
12-10

IF THEY GAVE MEDALS FOR LYING-HE'D BE COVERED WITH 'EM-
YES-ROSIE-I'M GLAD YOU CALLED UP-I WAS JUST LEAVING-THE BOSS AND I ARE JUST GOING OUT TO HAVE LUNCH TOGETHER-
IT DOESN'T DO ANY HARM TO PRETEND TO ROSIE-THAT THE BOSS AND I ARE CHUMMY--I WANT HER TO THINK THAT I'M IMPORTANT IN THIS FIRM--
GOING OUT-MISSIE?
YES-DORA-ARCHIE IS OUT TO LUNCH-SO I'LL SNEAK IN-TO HIS OFFICE TO LEAVE A LITTLE PRESENT FOR HIM-
Copr. 1939, King Features Syndicate, Inc., World rights reserved
NOW-LET'S SEE WHAT MY LANDLADY HAS WRAPPED UP FOR MY LUNCH TODAY-
12-17
?
HUH-WELL-DOES THE BOSS SIT ON THIS SIDE OF THE DESK FOR LUNCH? I'LL NOT DISTURB YOU-GOOD-BYE-
NOW-FOLKS-WE ARE ON THE EDGE OF THE GRAND CANYON-
MOTHER-DO YOU THINK YOU CAN HANDLE THAT DONKEY?
WHY NOT? I'VE TAKEN CARE OF YOUR FATHER FOR YEARS-
WE'RE REALLY ON A BRIDAL TOUR-WHAT? CLEVER JOKE-DON'T YOU THINK?
REALLY-LORD-WORTHNOTTEN-THE THINGS YOU SAY ARE SO WITTY-
IS THIS THE PLACE THERE IS SO MUCH COMMENT ABOUT THROWING OLD RAZOR BLADES?
YEAH-AN' ALL THE TIME-HALF-WITTED-
FATHER-DON'T BE SO RUDE-
HEAVENS! I THINK I'M GOING TO FAINT-
WELL-YOU HAD BETTER THINK TWICE-IF YOU FALL OFF THAT MULE-YOU'LL ROLL FOR MILES-
THIS IS JOLLY SPORT-
OH-I WISH THIS WAS OVER-
IF YOU SLIP-IT WILL BE ALL OVER-
ISN'T IT GORGEOUS? I'M SO AWED-WHY-IT'S BEAUTIFUL--I THINK I'LL SING-
BY GOLLY-WE MADE IT-
WHY SPOIL IT?
BUT-MOTHER-WHY SING?
MOTHER-WHAT'S THE IDEA OF BURSTING INTO SONG? DO YOU THINK THIS IS THE HOLLYWOOD BOWL?
I THINK I'LL GO OVER AN' HOLD TH' MULES-
12-17
UGH-NO PLACE INDIAN CAN GO TO HAVE PEACE-
I WISH I HAD MY BOW AND ARROW-
HEAP LOT UM NOISE IN UM SQUAW-
WHAT'S THE MATTER? HUSBAND BEATUM YOU?
HIRE UM HALL-
THESE INDIANS MUST KNOW WHAT REAL SINGING IS-
QUIET!!
UGH-HEAP LOT UM RACKET MAKE SICK INDIAN-

I'VE GOT TEN BUCKS TO BLOW IN ON ROSIE-THIS EVENING-
I'LL DRIVE UP IN A TAXI-THEN TAKE HER TO A SHOW AND SUPPER-
IS THAT THE CITY SLICKER YOU INTEND TO MARRY?
ARCHIE DARLING-MEET MY AUNT AND UNCLE FROM PUMPKIN CORNERS-
WAL-YOUNG FELLAR-WHILE TH' GALS ARE CHATTIN' WE CAN HAVE A GAME OF CHECKS-
WAL-IF YOU'D RATHER-WE'LL PLAY CARDS--CYNTHIA IS NOT IN FAVOR OF IT FOR ME-
WELL-IT'S BETTER THAN CHECKERS-
WAL-SON-WHAT ARE YOU GOIN' TO DO NOW? I'M WAITING-
PLAY THIS HAND-THEN I'M GOING HOME-
I SHOULD HAVE HELD OUT A DIME CARFARE-NOW I'VE GOT TO WALK HOME-WHAT A SAP I'VE BEEN-
12-24
WELL-NOW-I HAVE ALL THE PLACES OF INTEREST WE ARE TO VISIT HERE IN NEW YORK-WE WILL FIRST GO FER A STROLL ON FIFTH AVENUE-
OH-THAT WILL BE JOLLY-
I'M DYING TO SEE THE AQUARIUM-AMERICANS TALK SO MUCH OF THE POOR FISH-
COME NOW-CHILDREN WE MUST START IF WE INTEND TO SEE A LOT OF THE CITY-
WE MUST TAKE A LIFT ON ONE OF THOSE TRAMS-
THOSE ARE BUSES-NOW-TEN BLOCKS FROM HERE IS UNION SQUARE-
DAUGHTER-JUST LOOK AT THAT SPORT JACKET-
MOTHER-IT'S JUST WHAT I WANT-I'LL MEET YOU FOLKS AT UNION SQUARE-
THIS IS OUR GLORIOUS FIFTH AVENUE-
BY JOVE-THE PEOPLE IN THE TOPS OF THOSE BIG BUILDINGS PRACTICALLY ARE OUT OF TOWN-
YES-AND A LOT OF 'EM ARE OUT OF FUNDS-
NOW WHAT?
WHAT PRICE HATS-
LOOK AT THAT DARLING HAT-I MUST GO IN-YOU TWO RUN ALONG-I'LL MEET YOU AT UNION SQUARE-
NOW-DON'T GET EXCITED-MR. JIGGS-YOU HAVE BEEN MARRIED LONG ENOUGH TO KNOW WOMEN-
YOU MEAN-LONG ENOUGH NOT TO KNOW THEM-
IT IS TOO BAD THEY MISSED ALL THIS EXCITEMENT ON THE AVENUE-
YES-BUT THEY WON'T MISS A THING IN THEM STORES-
BY JOVE-THERE'S A LONDON PIPE SHOP-DO YOU MIND?-I WANT TO LOOK AT SOME BRIERS-
I'LL MEET YOU AT UNION SQUARE-
AT TH' RATE WE ARE GOING-IT WILL TAKE US SIXTY YEARS TO SEE NEW YORK-
?
I LEFT HIM TO GO TAKE A LOOK AT SOME PIPES-
AND I WENT TO UNION SQUARE-BUT I COULDN'T FIND HIM-I HOPE HE ISN'T LOST-
HE CERTAINLY CANNOT BE SIGHT-SEEING AT THIS HOUR OF THE NIGHT-
12-24

YES-DARLING-I'D LOVE TO COME DOWN AND SEE YOUR NEW OFFICE-I'LL LEAVE RIGHT NOW-DEAREST-GOOD-BYE-SWEETHEART-
GOSH-OH-GEE-I FORGOT-I'VE GOT TO GO RIGHT OVER WITH A BUNDLE TO MR KEN TELLYOU-I'LL GET NORMAN TO HELP ME OUT-
NOW-LISTEN-HERE'S A DIME-THE BOSS WON'T BE IN ALL DAY-SO WHEN MY SWEETIE CALLS-TAKE HER INTO THE BOSS' OFFICE AND TELL HER IT'S MINE-I WILL BE BACK IN A FEW MINUTES SO TELL HER TO WAIT FOR ME IN THERE-
WHEN I TOOK THIS JOB-THEY ASKED ME IF I WAS HONEST-
THANK GOODNESS THAT'S DONE, NOW TO GET BACK TO MY OFFICE TO SEE ROSIE-
WHERE IS SHE?
BOY-WAS SHE SORE-I TOOK HER IN THE BOSS' OFFICE -- YOU SEE-I FERGOT THE BOSS HAS TWO PICTURES OF DAMES ON HIS DESK-YER SWEETIE TOOK ONE LOOK-BOY-OH-BOY-SHE WENT OUT OF HERE SO FAST-SHE MUST BE HOME BY NOW-I DON'T CARE WHERE SHE LIVES--
Copr. 1939, King Features Syndicate, Inc., World rights reserved
12-31

WELL--HERE IS BROADWAY-THE GREAT WHITE WAY-THE RIALTO OF AMERICA-WHAT DO YOU THINK OF IT?
IT'S ALL RIGHT-I SUPPOSE-IF ONE LIKES ELECTRIC LIGHT BULBS-
THE CONVICT OR TIME ON MY HANDS
NOW-HERE WE ARE IN TH' HEART OF BEEKMAN PLACE-WHICH REMINDS ME-I USED TO KNOW A COP ON THIS BEAT-A COP, YOU KNOW IS A POLICEMAN--
HOW CAN A COP BE A POLICEMAN? A POLICEMAN IS REALLY A BOBBY-BUT NO MATTER-CONTINUE-
THIS IS THE HUDSON RIVER-THERE'S THE PALISADES ON THE NEW JERSEY SIDE AND IF YOU LOOK AHEAD FOR ABOUT TEN MILES YOU KIN SEE YONKERS-
REALLY? AND WHAT ARE YONKERS-MAY I ASK?

THIS IS THE SUBWAY-YOU CAN RIDE ALL DAY ON A NICKEL-
IT MUST BE QUITE TEDIOUS SITTING ON A NICKEL-I'LL JUST GO AND TAKE A LOOK-

UPTOWN

IT'S NEARLY MIDNIGHT-WHERE IS HE?? WHY DID YOU LET LORD WORTHNOTTEN OUT OF YOUR SIGHT?
HE WENT DOWN TO TAKE A LOOK AT TH' SUBWAY-I WAITED TWO HOURS AN' HE NEVER CAME UP-
THERE'S THE 'PHONE-IT MAY BE MY DARLING-
Copr. 1939, King Features Syndicate, Inc., World rights reserved

YES-PRECIOUS DARLING-WHERE ARE YOU? WE'VE BEEN FRANTIC ABOUT YOUR WHERE-ABOUTS-WHAT HAPPENED IN THE SUBWAY?

I HAVEN'T THE SLIGHTEST IDEA-THE FIRST THING I KNEW-I WAS ON A TRAIN AND BEFORE I COULD MASH MY WAY OUT I FIND I'M ON AN ISLAND THAT IS NAMED AFTER A FELLOW NAMED CONEY-EATING HOT CANINES IS QUITE PREDOMINANT HERE-AM I STILL IN AMERICA?
12-31

YES-ROSIE-MY DOVE-THE BOSS IS GOIN' TO FIRE THE MANAGER-THE OFFICE BOY TOLD ME SECRETLY-AM I HAPPY-DEAR-
THAT MEANS YOU WILL BE THE NEW MANAGER-BABY-IT WON'T BE LONG BEFORE YOU ARE PRESIDENT-
I'LL BET HE'S FIRING HIM JUST TO MAKE YOU MANAGER-
OH-NO DOUBT ABOUT THAT-
I GUESS THE BOSS WILL TELL ME ABOUT IT SOMETIME TODAY-
Copr. 1940, King Features Syndicate, Inc., World rights reserved
DID YOU FIND OUT JUST WHEN THE BOSS IS GOING TO LET HIM OUT?
YEP-JUST AS SOON AS HE GETS HIS AFFAIRS STRAIGHTENED OUT-
!
BEFORE HE LEAVES THE BOSS WANTS HIM TO FIRE YOU-
1-7
NO-HUBBY DEAR-I'M NOT GOING SIGHTSEEING TODAY-I HAVE A NUMBER OF LETTERS TO WRITE-SO YOU AND DADDY RUN ALONG-
SORRY-BUT I MUST SEE NEW YORK IF IT TAKES TWO DAYS-
NEVER MIND-DAUGHTER KNOWS NEW YORK QUITE WELL-SHE WAS BORN IN BROOKLYN-
WELL-WHERE DO YOU THINK YOU ARE GOING AND WHAT GAVE YOU THE IDEA THAT I AM NOT GOING WITH YOU?
THOSE ARE YOUR QUESTIONS-YOU HAD BETTER ANSWER THEM-
THERE ISN'T AN ANSWER-SHE'S GOIN' WITH US-
THAT'S THE MARVELOUS SKY-LINE OF LOWER MANHATTAN-WE ARE VIEWING IT FROM THE BROOKLYN SIDE-IT IS STUPENDOUSLY COLOSSAL WHAT SAY YOU? WE'LL GO RIGHT OVER THERE NOW-
MANHATTAN?? IS IT NEAR TO NEW YORK? IT MUST BE QUITE DIFFICULT TO BECOME ACQUAINTED IN SUCH A VAST METROPOLIS-
YOU SAID IT-WHY-YOU COULD BE A GREAT MOVIE STAR AN' WALK ANYWHERE AND NO ONE WOULD EVEN NOTICE YOU-
HOWDY-JIGGS-
WELCOME BACK TO THE OLD STREET-
HYA-JIGGS-
HEY-JIGGS-
BY JOVE-YOUR NAME MUST HAVE LEAKED OUT SOMEHOW-
HELLO-MR. JIGGS-
LET'S GET OUT OF HERE-I TOLD YOU NOT TO COME DOWN IN THE SLUMS-
HYA-JIGGS-
HY-JIGGS-
HELLO-JIGGS-
LET'S GET OVER TO PARK AVENUE-WHERE I'LL FEEL MORE AT HOME-IT MUST BE DREADFUL LIVING IN SUCH A NEIGHBORHOOD-
IT WAS-I MEAN-LET'S GIT A CAB-
I RATHER LIKED THAT CONGESTED LANE-THEY ALL SEEMED SO HAPPY-
1-7
HULLO-MAGGIE-HOW DOES IT FEEL TO LIVE ON TH' OTHER SIDE OF THE RAILROAD TRACKS-NOW?
MY-ISN'T SHE THE PRETTY BIRD SINCE SHE WORKED HERE IN THE GAY NINETIES-
THEY ARE NOT ALL FRIENDS OF YOURS-MAGGIE-SOME OF THEM ARE RELATIVES-
WE MISS YOU-AND WE MISSED A LOT OF SHIRTS WHEN YOU LEFT-
WE MUST BE GETTING NEAR PARK AVENUE-
RIPPIN LAUNDRY
"BRING IN YOUR TORN SHIRTS-WE'LL FINISH THEM-"
Copr. 1940, King Features Syndicate, Inc., World rights reserved.

ARCHIE-DARLING-I'VE GOT TO GO OVER TO AUNT EMMA'S HOUSE TONIGHT-JUST THINK-I WON'T SEE YOU UNTIL TO-MORROW-IT WILL SEEM LIKE YEARS-MY LOVE-

THAT IS TOO BAD-SUGAR PLUM-I DID SO WANT TO TAKE YOU OUT TONIGHT-GEE-I'LL MISS NOT SEE-ING YOU-YES-DARLING-I AM LEAVING FOR MY OFFICE NOW-

GOSH-IT'S LUCKY FOR ME ROSIE CALLED OFF OUR DATE-I HAVE GOT ONLY SIXTY CENTS TO LAST ME FOR TH' REST OF THE WEEK-

MISS ROSIE 'PHONED AND SAID SHE HAS TO SEE YOU-SO SHE IS ON HER WAY DOWN HERE SO YOU CAN TAKE HER TO LUNCH-

?

I'D LIKE TO GET FIVE ON THIS WATCH-

1-14

WELL-THIS IS THE SOLDIERS' MONUMENT ON RIVERSIDE DRIVE-AND IF YOU FOLKS DON'T MIND I'M GOING BACK TO THE HOTEL-I AM PRETTY TIRED-

VERY WELL-DAUGHTER AND I MUST DO SOME SHOPPING-

I'LL GO WITH THE LADIES-DO YOU MIND?

WE'LL BE BACK TO THE HOTEL EARLY-DADDY-

AH-IT'S A RELIEF TO GIT BACK AND TAKE A NAP-

WHAT'S THAT? YES-THIS IS MR. JIGGS-YOU SAY YOU HAVE SOME PACKAGES FOR MY WIFE? WELL-SEND THEM UP--

VERY GOOD-MR. JIGGS-RIGHT AWAY-

SAY-HOW ABOUT A LITTLE ATTENTION?

HUH-YOU'RE GETTING AS LITTLE AS HE CAN GIVE YOU-

HERE'S YOUR PACKAGE-MR. JIGGS-

HERE-ME LAD-HERE IS A QUARTER FOR YOU-

A PACKAGE FOR YOU-SIR-

I SUPPOSE YOU WOULD HAVE BROKEN AN ARM IF YOU HAD TO CARRY THE OTHER PACKAGE THAT OTHER KID HAD-

PACKAGE FOR YOU-

HERE-TOO-

PACKAGE-SIR-AND I CAN CHANGE A TEN-DOLLAR BILL-

I SUPPOSE IF IT WAS A LARGE BUNDLE-YOU'D TEAR IT APART AND EACH BRING UP A PIECE OF IT-

ARCHIE-DARLING-I WANT YOU TO CALL EARLY-DEAR-AS I'M GOING TO COOK A NICE DINNER FOR YOU-
MY DARLING IS GOING TO COOK DINNER FOR ME-MY LANDLADY IS OUT SO I'LL PRACTISE SETTING A TABLE-
I WANT TO BE A GREAT HELP-MATE TO ROSIE WHEN WE GET MARRIED-
I'LL PRACTISE A BIT-THEN WHEN I GET TO HER HOUSE-I'LL SHOW HER THAT I'LL FALL INTO THE WAYS OF KEEPING HOUSE-
I WONDER IF THE BOSS WAS RIGHT THE OTHER DAY WHEN HE SAID I WAS CLUMSY?
Copr. 1940, King Features Syndicate, Inc., World rights reserved
1-21

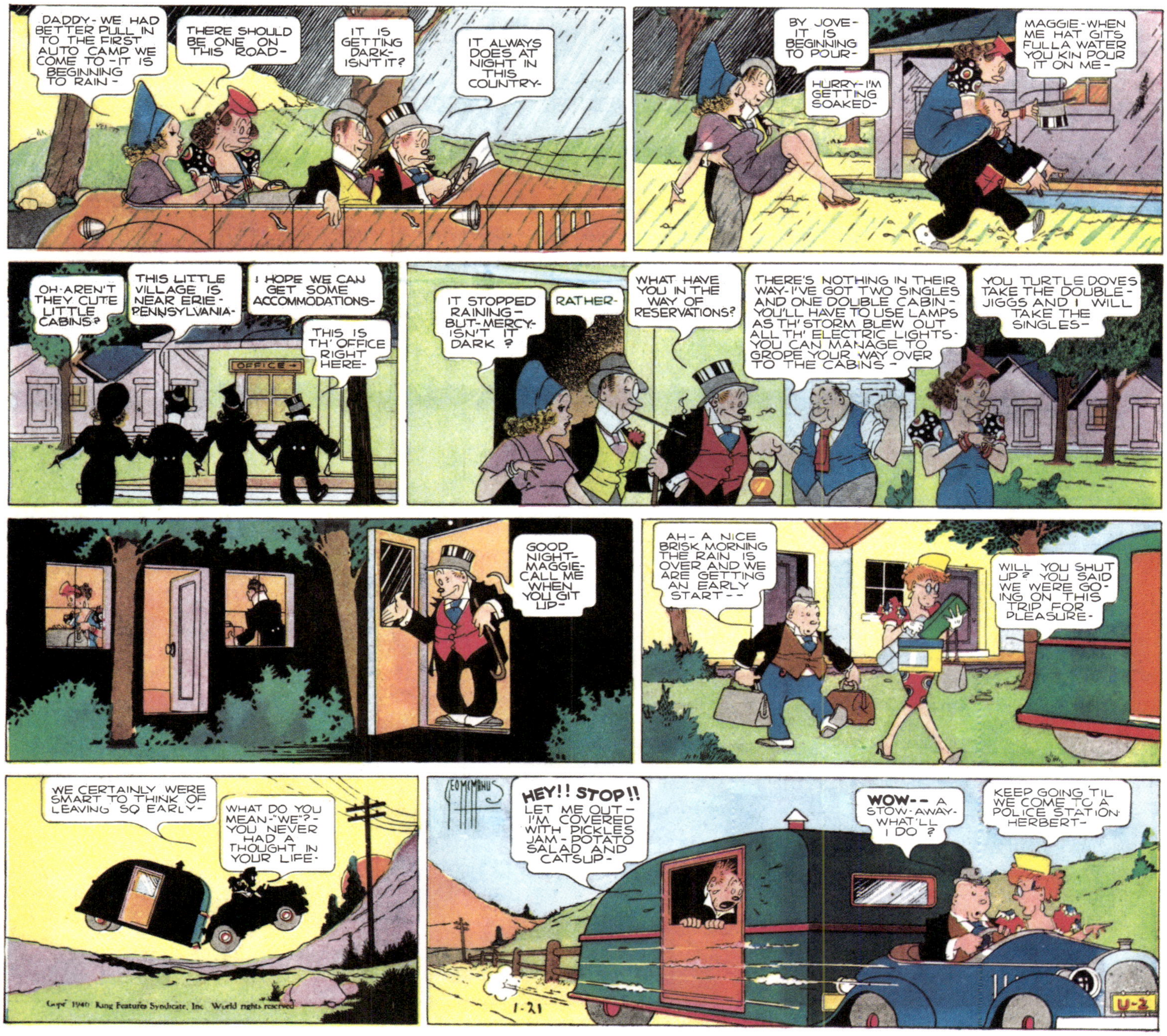

DADDY-WE HAD BETTER PULL IN TO THE FIRST AUTO CAMP WE COME TO-IT IS BEGINNING TO RAIN-
THERE SHOULD BE ONE ON THIS ROAD-
IT IS GETTING DARK-ISN'T IT?
IT ALWAYS DOES AT NIGHT IN THIS COUNTRY-
BY JOVE-IT IS BEGINNING TO POUR-
HURRY-I'M GETTING SOAKED-
MAGGIE-WHEN ME HAT GITS FULLA WATER YOU KIN POUR IT ON ME-
OH-AREN'T THEY CUTE LITTLE CABINS?
THIS LITTLE VILLAGE IS NEAR ERIE-PENNSYLVANIA-
I HOPE WE CAN GET SOME ACCOMMODATIONS-
THIS IS TH' OFFICE RIGHT HERE-
OFFICE
IT STOPPED RAINING-BUT-MERCY-ISN'T IT DARK?
RATHER-
WHAT HAVE YOU IN THE WAY OF RESERVATIONS?
THERE'S NOTHING IN THEIR WAY-I'VE GOT TWO SINGLES AND ONE DOUBLE CABIN-YOU'LL HAVE TO USE LAMPS AS TH' STORM BLEW OUT ALL TH' ELECTRIC LIGHTS-YOU CAN MANAGE TO GROPE YOUR WAY OVER TO THE CABINS-
YOU TURTLE DOVES TAKE THE DOUBLE-JIGGS AND I WILL TAKE THE SINGLES-
GOOD NIGHT-MAGGIE-CALL ME WHEN YOU GIT UP-
AH-A NICE BRISK MORNING THE RAIN IS OVER AND WE ARE GETTING AN EARLY START--
WILL YOU SHUT UP? YOU SAID WE WERE GOING ON THIS TRIP FOR PLEASURE-

WE CERTAINLY WERE SMART TO THINK OF LEAVING SO EARLY-
WHAT DO YOU MEAN-"WE"?-YOU NEVER HAD A THOUGHT IN YOUR LIFE-
Copr 1940 King Features Syndicate, Inc. World rights reserved

GEO MCMANUS
HEY!! STOP!! LET ME OUT-I'M COVERED WITH PICKLES JAM-POTATO SALAD AND CATSUP-
WOW-- A STOW-AWAY-WHAT'LL I DO?
KEEP GOING 'TIL WE COME TO A POLICE STATION HERBERT-
1-21
U-2

WELL - COME - CHILDREN - WE MUST SEE THE FALLS - WHERE IS DADDY?
YES - WHERE IS THAT WANDERING FOOL?
HE SAID HE'D GO AHEAD AND MEET US AT THE FALLS -
1.
SO - THIS IS NIAGARA FALLS - HUH - I SUPPOSE THESE LOVE-SICK HONEYMOONERS THINK THIS WORLD IS MADE OF MUSH - BOY - OH - BOY - WAIT 'TIL THEY COME OUT OF THAT TRANCE -
2.
BY GOLLY - THEM COOERS REMIND ME OF THE OLD DAYS WHEN I USED TO GIT IN A BOAT AN' JUST DRIFT AN' DREAM OF TH' HAPPY DAYS TO COME -
3.
LITTLE DID I KNOW THAT WHEN I WALKED UP THE LADDER OF MATRIMONY - I WAS HEADING FOR A FALL -
4.
5.

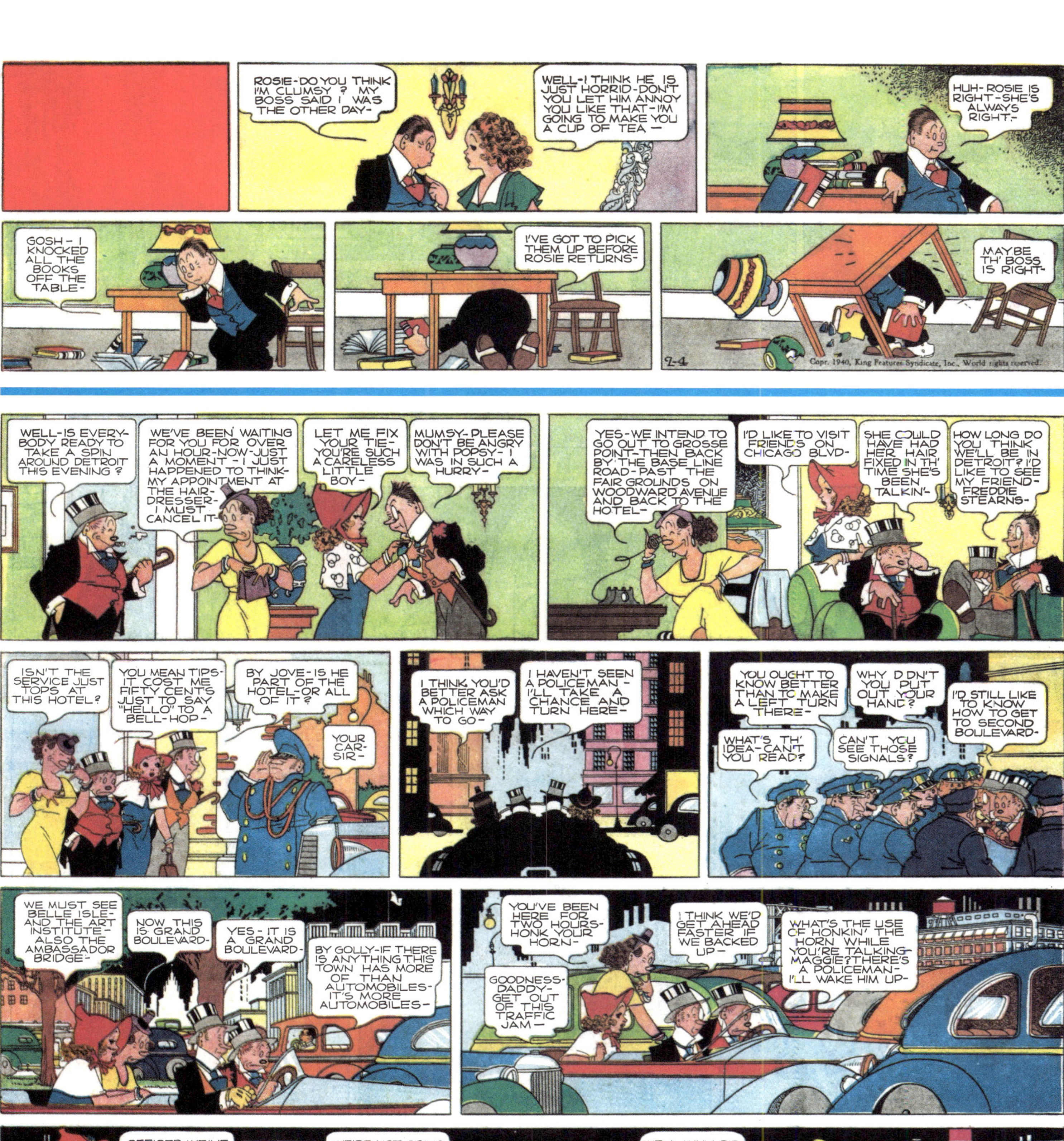

ROSIE-DO YOU THINK I'M CLUMSY? MY BOSS SAID I WAS THE OTHER DAY-
WELL-I THINK HE IS JUST HORRID-DON'T YOU LET HIM ANNOY YOU LIKE THAT-I'M GOING TO MAKE YOU A CUP OF TEA-
HUH-ROSIE IS RIGHT-SHE'S ALWAYS RIGHT-
GOSH-I KNOCKED ALL THE BOOKS OFF THE TABLE-
I'VE GOT TO PICK THEM UP BEFORE ROSIE RETURNS-
MAYBE TH' BOSS IS RIGHT-
2-4
Copr. 1940, King Features Syndicate, Inc., World rights reserved.
WELL-IS EVERYBODY READY TO TAKE A SPIN AROUND DETROIT THIS EVENING?
WE'VE BEEN WAITING FOR YOU FOR OVER AN HOUR-NOW-JUST A MOMENT-I JUST HAPPENED TO THINK-MY APPOINTMENT AT THE HAIR-DRESSER-I MUST CANCEL IT-
LET ME FIX YOUR TIE-YOU'RE SUCH A CARELESS LITTLE BOY-
MUMSY-PLEASE DON'T BE ANGRY WITH POPSY-I WAS IN SUCH A HURRY-
YES-WE INTEND TO GO OUT TO GROSSE POINT-THEN BACK BY THE BASE LINE ROAD-PAST THE FAIR GROUNDS ON WOODWARD AVENUE AND BACK TO THE HOTEL-
I'D LIKE TO VISIT FRIENDS ON CHICAGO BLVD-
SHE COULD HAVE HAD HER HAIR FIXED IN TH' TIME SHE'S BEEN TALKIN'-
HOW LONG DO YOU THINK WE'LL BE IN DETROIT? I'D LIKE TO SEE MY FRIEND-FREDDIE STEARNS-
ISN'T THE SERVICE JUST TOPS AT THIS HOTEL?
YOU MEAN TIPS-IT COST ME FIFTY CENTS JUST TO SAY "HELLO" TO A BELL-HOP-
BY JOVE-IS HE PART OF THE HOTEL-OR ALL OF IT?
YOUR CAR-SIR-
I THINK YOU'D BETTER ASK A POLICEMAN WHICH WAY TO GO-
I HAVEN'T SEEN A POLICEMAN-I'LL TAKE A CHANCE AND TURN HERE-
YOU OUGHT TO KNOW BETTER THAN TO MAKE A LEFT TURN THERE-
WHY DIDN'T YOU PUT OUT YOUR HAND?
I'D STILL LIKE TO KNOW HOW TO GET TO SECOND BOULEVARD-
WHAT'S TH' IDEA-CAN'T YOU READ?
CAN'T YOU SEE THOSE SIGNALS?
WE MUST SEE BELLE ISLE-AND THE ART INSTITUTE-ALSO THE AMBASSADOR BRIDGE-
NOW THIS IS GRAND BOULEVARD-
YES-IT IS A GRAND BOULEVARD-
BY GOLLY-IF THERE IS ANYTHING THIS TOWN HAS MORE OF THAN AUTOMOBILES-IT'S MORE AUTOMOBILES-
YOU'VE BEEN HERE FOR TWO HOURS-HONK YOUR HORN-
I THINK WE'D GET AHEAD FASTER IF WE BACKED UP-
WHAT'S THE USE OF HONKIN' THE HORN WHILE YOU'RE TALKING-MAGGIE? THERE'S A POLICEMAN-I'LL WAKE HIM UP-
GOODNESS-DADDY-GET OUT OF THIS TRAFFIC JAM-
OFFICER-WE'VE BEEN HERE FOUR HOURS-
CAN'T YOU MAKE THEM MOVE THEIR CARS?
WE'RE NOT GOING TO STAY HERE ALL NIGHT-WE WANT TO GIT HOME-
WELL-WHY DID YOU DRIVE IN HERE? THIS IS THE FREIGHT YARD OF THE DELAPID EIGHT AUTOMOBILE COMPANY-
GEO MC MANUS
2-4
Copr. 1940, King Features Syndicate, Inc., World rights reserved.

I'LL JUST FIX MYSELF A CUP OF COFFEE BEFORE I CALL ON ROSIE IF IT WASN'T FOR ROSIE - I WOULD GET SORE AT THE BOSS FER SAYIN' I WAS CLUMSY-
DARN IT- NOW I WONDER IF I'M GETTING CLUMSY JUST BECAUSE THE BOSS SAYS I AM?
NOW-LISTEN-ARCHIE DARLING-DON'T YOU LET ANYONE SAY YOU'RE CLUMSY-YOU ARE NOT-YOUR BOSS IS AN OLD GROUCH-
YOU'RE RIGHT-ROSIE - YOU KNOW I'M NOT CLUMSY-
BYE-BYE-MY PET-I'LL CALL YOU UP AS SOON AS I'M BACK AT THE OFFICE-
Copr. 1940, King Features Syndicate, Inc., World rights reserved.
2-11
I DIDN'T QUITE GET WHAT THE GUIDE SAID-WHO DID HE SAY WAS BURIED IN GRANT'S TOMB?
DOESN'T THE STATUE OF LIBERTY LOOK MAJESTIC OUT THERE ON BEDLOE'S ISLAND? NOW THAT IS THE BATTERY-AND THAT'S--
NEXT WE'LL GO TO SEE CENTRAL PARK-I'D LIKE TO KNOW HOW TO GIT THERE-BUT A NEW YORKER WOULDN'T KNOW-
I'M GLAD WE'RE BACK IN NEW YORK-THERE ARE SO MANY BEAUTIFUL THINGS TO SEE HERE-
YES-DEAREST-THAT IS FIFTH AVENUE AT FIFTY-NINTH STREET-
JIGGS!
BUT-MAGGIE-I'M JUST TAKIN' IN THE BEAUTY OF NEW YORK-
MOTHER-I'M NOT GOING DOWN THAT STREET-
ME EITHER-
BEASTLY DIRTY-WHAT?
I'LL STROLL IN A LITTLE WAY JUST TO GET SOME ATMOSPHERE OF THE STREET-
UMBRELLAS TRUNKS
DELICATESSEN
SOME ATMOSPHERE-
CLOAK SUITS
NEXT-WE'LL VISIT THE MUSEUM OF NATURAL HISTORY-I WISH DADDY WOULD HURRY BACK-
I THINK YOU HAD BETTER GO LOOK FOR HIM-
WELL-MAYBE IT'S BORING TO WAIT HERE-
I HOPE HE DIDN'T TURN OFF THIS STREET-
GRACIOUS-WHY DON'T THEY HURRY BACK?
LOOK-MOTHER-HERE COMES TWO FUNNY-LOOKING CREATURES-
HUBBY!
JIGGS!
VERY SPIRITED SALESMEN IN THAT STORE-DO YOU THINK I DID WRONG BY TAKING A BAT AND BALL INSTEAD OF A WHISTLE?
LEND ME THAT BAT-I'M GONNA GO AND GIT ME SUIT BACK-
GEO McMANUS
Copr. 1940, King Features Syndicate, Inc., World rights reserved.
2-11

ROSIE- I JUST BUMPED MY HEAD- NOW I AM BEGINNING TO THINK I'M AS CLUMSY AS MY BOSS SAYS I AM-
HONEY- PLEASE DON'T TALK LIKE THAT- YOU ARE JUST A DARLING LITTLE BOY- YOU MUST NOT THINK ANY SUCH THOUGHT-
I HOPE ROSIE IS RIGHT- BUT I DID BUMP MY HEAD- BUT AFTER ALL- ANYONE COULD DO THAT-
ROSIE IS RIGHT- I MUSTN'T THINK I'M CLUMSY- IT'S JUST MY IMAGINATION -
2-18
IT'S A NOTE FROM MY COUSIN LARRY- HE'S ONE OF THE BIG MEN WITH THE LITTUP COAL MINING COMPANY HERE NEAR PITTSBURGH-
HE MAY BE BIG BUT NOT IMPORTANT-
SHUT UP- YOU GO RIGHT OVER TO THE PRESIDENT'S OFFICE AND MEET HIM AND BRING HIM WITH YOU- INSIST ON HIM DINING HERE AT THE HOTEL WITH US TONIGHT-
IF HE'S LIKE TH' REST OF YOUR KIN- I'LL NOT HAVE TO INSIST-
TELL HIM TO COME AS HE IS- AS WE WILL NOT DRESS FOR DINNER- I HOPE HE INTRODUCES YOU TO THE PRESIDENT-
I HOPE SOME DAY WE WILL GIT TO A TOWN WHERE YOU HAVEN'T ANY RELATIVES-
YES- I'M GOING WITH YOU- MR. JIGGS- I'VE NEVER SEEN A COAL FACTORY-
REMEMBER- TREAT HIM LIKE ONE OF THE FAMILY-
BUT- MAGGIE- WHY START ARGUING WITH HIM?
WE'D LIKE TO SEE LARRY BARRY- WE UNDERSTAND HE'S NEXT TO THE PRESIDENT-
HE ISN'T THE ONLY ONE- WE'RE ALL NEXT TO HIM -- IF YOU WISH TO SEE LARRY BARRY- YOU WILL HAVE TO GO OVER TO THE MINE SHAFT OFFICE -
LARRY BARRY? HE'S DOWN IN MINE SHAFT NUMBER FIVE- I'LL GET A MAN TO TAKE YOU DOWN-
TAKE THESE TWO DOWN AN' BRING BACK TWO MULES-
NOW- WHAT DOES THAT MEAN?
ALL RIGHT- JOE-
WHAT AN EXTRAORDINARY PLACE TO WORK-
DON'T WORRY- YOU WON'T FIND HIM WORKING-
IS THAT HIM STANDING OVER THERE?
NO- THAT'S A MULE-
NO ONE EVER SAW HIM STANDIN' UP- I'LL FIND HIM ASLEEP SOME- WHERE -
I HOPE HE BRINGS THE PRESIDENT WITH HIM -
DO YOU THINK LARRY WILL KNOW YOU? YOU KNOW YOU HAVEN'T SEEN HIM IN YEARS-
BY JOVE- IT WAS A WEE BIT DUSTY IN HIS OFFICE-
WE HAD A HARD TIME GITTIN' IN TH' HOTEL LIKE THIS-
HELLO- MAGGIE- MITT ME- I HAVEN'T SEEN YOU SINCE I BROUGHT YOUR FATHER HOME IN A WHEEL-BARREL-
LARRY!
MERCY!
GEO McMANUS
2-18

ARCHIE-DARLING - YOU MUST STOP THINKING YOU'RE CLUMSY - YOU ARE JUST A SWEET-DARLING-LITTLE BOY-AND I LOVE YOU - YOU ARE NOT CLUMSY -
THANKS-DARLING - WHEN THINGS LOOK BLACK FOR ME - YOU ALWAYS CHEER ME UP -
HEY - YOU - CLUMSY FAT-HEAD - GET YOUR HAND OUT OF THE INK - WELL -
?
I'M GOING TO TAKE THIS VASE OUT OF THE WAY BEFORE YOU BREAK IT - I NEVER SAW SO CLUMSY A MAN
2.25
Copr 1940, King Features Syndicate, Inc., World rights reserved
IF YOU OPEN YOUR MOUTH AND SAY ONE WORD - I'LL HIT YOU WITH A CHAIR -
WE'LL BE RUNNING ALONG NOW AS HUBBY AND I HAVE SOME SHOPPING TO DO HERE IN PHILADELPHIA -
IT'S TOO BAD YOU'RE NOT GOING WITH US - PHILADELPHIA IS A GREAT HISTORICAL SPOT IN OUR AMERICAN HISTORY - I HAVE ALL TH' DATA ON IT -
DON'T ALWAYS BE TELLING PEOPLE WHAT TO DO - GET YOUR HAT - I WANT TO SEE THE CITY -
I NEVER SAW SUCH A MAN - BUTTING INTO EVERYONE'S AFFAIRS - SPEAK UP - WHAT BUILDING IS THAT ? WHAT'S IT SAY ON THE PAPER ?
THAT'S CARPENTERS' HALL WHERE THE CONSTITUTION WAS FRAMED -
TH' CELLAR WAS AN AMMUNITION MAGAZINE IN THE WAR FOR FREEDOM - I SAID - FREEDOM -
GREAT HEAVENS - WHY DIDN'T YOU BRUSH YOUR SUIT THIS MORNING ? I NEVER SAW ANYONE SO UNTIDY -
THIS - NOW - IS INDEPENDENCE SQUARE - A HISTORIC SPOT IN THE LAND OF THE FREE -
THIS IS THE HOME OF BETSY ROSS - WHO MADE OUR GREAT FLAG OF FREEDOM -
DIDN'T I TELL YOU NOT TO WEAR THAT OLD TIE ? WILL YOU EVER MIND ?
AND THIS IS INDEPENDENCE HALL - IN HERE IS THE FAMOUS LIBERTY BELL WHICH RANG FOR LIBERTY AND FREEDOM IN 1776 -
BY THE WAY - DID YOU MAIL THOSE LETTERS I GAVE YOU YESTERDAY ? STOP TRYING TO TALK WITH A CIGAR IN YOUR MOUTH - AND STRAIGHTEN YOUR HAT -
THIS IS THE INTERIOR OF INDEPENDENCE HALL - IN THIS ROOM THE DECLARATION OF INDEPENDENCE WAS SIGNED - THE BEGINNING OF LIBERTY -
WILL YOU PIPE DOWN THAT FOG HORN VOICE OF YOURS ? AND DON'T TURN YOUR BACK TO ME - DIDN'T I TELL YOU TO GET A HAIR - CUT YESTERDAY ?
NOW - THIS IS THE LIBERTY BELL - THAT RANG OUT PROCLAIMIN' LIBERTY FOR ALL MEN -
DON'T POINT - WILL YOU NEVER HAVE ANY MANNERS ?
GEO MC MANUS
WELL - MOTHER - DID YOU HAVE AN ENJOYABLE DAY ?
MARVELOUS CITY - DON'T YOU THINK ?
THE THINGS I SAW TODAY HELD ME SPEECHLESS - IT'S WONDERFUL TO LIVE IN A FREE COUNTRY LIKE OURS WHERE EVERYONE CAN COME AND GO AS THEY PLEASE AND DO WHAT THEY LIKE -
OH - NOT EVERY - ONE -
Copr 1940, King Features Syndicate, Inc., World rights reserved
2.25

I'VE CALLED ARCHIE AT LEAST TWENTY TIMES AND HIS 'PHONE IS ALWAYS BUSY- I'LL TRY AGAIN -HELLO-
STILL BUSY- I'VE BEEN TRYING TWO HOURS AND IT IS ALWAYS BUSY- WELL-HERE GOES - I'LL TRY AGAIN -
GOSH- WHO CAN ROSIE BE TALKING TO ALL THIS TIME ?
STILL BUSY- I'LL TRY AGAIN- GOSH-THREE HOURS AND SHE IS STILL TALKING -
GRACIOUS- HE'S STILL BUSY- I JUST KNOW HE IS TALKING TO A GIRL- NO ONE COULD TALK BUSINESS THAT LONG -
I'LL TRY HIM JUST ONCE MORE-
WELL- I GIVE UP- SHE MUST BE TALKING TO ONE OF THOSE FOOTBALL PLAYERS SHE MET, LAST FALL- BAH-
Copr. 1940, King Features Syndicate, Inc., World rights reserved.
3-3
MAGGIE-I LIKE IT HERE AT LAKE PLACID -BUT I DO THINK IT'S A MISTAKE FOR ME TO TRY TO SKATE --
DON'T BE SILLY - IT WILL GIVE YOU A LOT OF GRACE-
STAND STILL- YOU MAKE ME NERVOUS-
BY GOLLY- YOUR NERVES ARE JUMPIN' -
THEY'RE OFFERING PRIZES FOR THE BEST SKATERS-
WE WON'T HAVE TO WORRY ABOUT THAT-
THERE GOES A VEST BUTTON-
MAGGIE - WHAT DOES PLACID MEAN ?
IT MEANS CALM AND PEACEFUL-
WE MUST BE IN THE WRONG PLACE-
BY GOLLY- WE ARE GONNA BUMP INTO THE CLUB - HOUSE - AN' IF WE MISS IT - WE'LL BE IN MONTREAL-
YOU GO AHEAD AND OPEN THE DOOR-
WELL- WE'RE AMONG THE TROPHIES-
3-3
Copr. 1940, King Features Syndicate, Inc., World rights reserved.
MOTHER - NOW YOU SHOULD HAVE KNOWN BETTER THAN TO TRY TO SKATE -
HOW LONG WERE YOU ON THE ICE MR. JIGGS?
ABOUT EVERY FIVE SECONDS - AN' ME SKATES TOUCHED THE ICE ONCE - I STILL THINK ONE OF THEM TROPHIES IS STICKIN' IN ME BACK-
TO ADD INSULT TO INJURY- ONE OF THE JUDGES GAVE ME A CUP FOR ACROBATIC SKATING -
GEO McMANUS

OH-ARCHIE, DARLING-WHAT WILL I DO? I CAN'T THINK OF YOU BEING AWAY FROM ME-I THINK YOUR BOSS IS HORRID TO SEND YOU AWAY-I'M SO UNHAPPY-
DON'T CRY-ROSIE-MY BEAUTIFUL-BE BRAVE LIKE ME-I THINK OF YOU EVERY MINUTE-I'LL WRITE YOU EVERY HOUR AND 'PHONE YOU ALL THE TIME-OH-THIS IS TERRIBLE-OH-MY-
YEP-TH' BOSS IS SENDING ME OUT ON THE ROAD-
WELL-THINK OF THE CHANCE HE'S GIVING YOU-YOU'RE IN LINE FOR PROMOTION-
WHAT GOOD IS THAT WHEN I'M AWAY FROM MY ROSIE?
HOW LONG ARE YOU TO BE ON TH' ROAD?
TWO DAYS-
3-10
Copr 1940, King Features Syndicate, Inc., World rights reserved
AT LAST WE ARE ON OUR WAY TO FLORIDA-I'M JUST DYING TO GET INTO MY NEW BATHING-SUIT-
I'M ANXIOUS TO GET THERE AS I WANT TO BUY SOME ALLI-GATORS-I HAVEN'T HAD ON SPATS SINCE I LEFT LONDON-
IT WILL BE EVER SO DELIGHTFUL TO GET IN THE SOCIAL WHIRL OF FLORIDA-I JUST KNOW MY SOCIAL CALENDAR WILL BE CROWDED WITH APPOINTMENTS-
I WONDER IF DUGAN STILL HAS HIS OLD PLACE IN TAMPA?
I HOPE MIAMI AND PALM BEACH HAS SOME GUYS OF ME KIND-I UNDERSTAND ALL OF THEM SOCIETY DAMES LOOK THROUGH GLASSES ON A STICK AN' DRINK FROM MINIATURE COFFEE CUPS-
WELL-WELL-IF IT ISN'T "BLAB-MOUTH" O'GINITY-TH' LAST TIME I SAW YOU-YOU WAS IN A PATROL WAGON-WHEN DID YOU DECIDE TO GO TO SEA?
I DECIDED WHEN I GOT OUT OF JAIL THAT THEY CAN'T SEND A PATROL WAGON FOR ME WHEN I'M ON THE OCEAN-
I EXPECT TO HAVE A GRAND TIME IN FLORIDA-EVERYTHING WILL BE SWELL-IF I KIN JUST AVOID THE SOCIETY CROWDS-
OH-THAT'S EASY-I DIDN'T HAVE ANY TROUBLE KEEPIN' AWAY FROM THEM-
JIGGS-
NOW-YOU SIT THERE-DON'T YOU MOVE 'TIL I RETURN-I MUST SEE THE HEAD STEWARD AND HAVE HIM PUT US AT THE CAPTAIN'S TABLE-
THAT MEANS I WON'T GIT A CHANCE TO DRINK OUT OF A SAUCER THE WHOLE TRIP-
TELL ME-IS LEM UNNADE STILL LOOKIN' FER WORK AN' HOPIN' HE WON'T FIND IT? I MISS TH' OLD GANG-
REMEMBER "BUTCH" CHERSHOP? HE GOT A JOB IN THE CITY JAIL SO HE COULD BE NEAR TO HIS FATHER-
GEO McMANUS
OH-OH-THIS REMINDS ME OF MY HOME-SEE YOU LATER-JIGGS-
YOU INSECT-WHY DON'T YOU TRY TO BE SOMEBODY? GET UP OUT OF THAT CHAIR-
3-10
NOW-YOU STAY IN HERE-AND TO BE SURE YOU DO-I'M GOIN' TO LOCK YOU IN-YOU KNOW I HAVE A WEAK HEART-STILL YOU ACT THIS WAY-
THAT WEAKNESS HASN'T SPREAD INTO YER RIGHT ARM-I KIN TELL YOU THAT-
YEH-DAVE BUILT A BOWLIN' ALLEY AND TOM HAS CHARGE OF THE PINS-
NOW GO ON WITH YER STORY-I HEARD THAT TOM HANJERRY WUZ SETTIN' 'EM UP IN DAVE'S PLACE-IS THAT TRUE ABOUT THAT CHEAP GUY?
Copr 1940, King Features Syndicate, Inc., World rights reserved

WHY-YES-ARCHIE DARLING I'LL MEET YOU IN FRONT OF THE POST OFFICE -FINE-I'D LOVE TO HAVE LUNCH WITH MY BABY BOY-YOU KNOW I LOVE YOU-

I'LL MEET YOU IN TWENTY MINUTES-IT'S ABOUT A MILE FROM MY OFFICE-

I'LL GO IN NOW AN' TELL THE BOSS-MY WORK IS ALL FINISHED AND I WANT TO GO OUT TO BUY A NEW SUIT-
Copr. 1940, King Features Syndicate, Inc., World rights reserved

WELL-IF YOU'VE NOTHING TO DO-JUST ASSORT MY MAIL-AND WHEN YOU FINISH-I'LL HAVE SOMETHING ELSE FOR YOU TO DO -
YES-SIR-

GOSH-WHAT CAN I DO? ROSIE IS WAITING AN' I CAN'T PHONE HER-

BY GOLLY-JIGGS-I'M SURPRISED TO SEE YOU IN WASHINGTON -
AN' I'M JUST AS SURPRISED TO SEE YOU OUT OF JAIL-DINNY-

I'LL TAKE YOU OVER TO McNACKNEY'S PLACE-A LOT OF SENATORS GO BY HIS PLACE-AN' DO THEY GO BY--
I PROMISED TO MEET MAGGIE NEAR THE CAPITOL-SO I WON'T BE ABLE TO STAY LONG-

WELL-WHAT ARE WE WAITIN' FOR? WHO'S BUYIN'?
IF IT ISN'T DAN-IT'S GLAD I AM TO SEE YOU-WHAT'S YOUR BROTHER DOING NOW?
SIX MONTHS-HE'S A FINE BOY-HE WILL BE OUT IN FOUR ON GOOD BEHAVIOR-BUT TELL ME ABOUT YOU-

NOW-WHERE'S THAT BIG WALRUS? I TOLD HIM TO MEET US RIGHT HERE-WE HAVE LOOKED ALL OVER-BUT NO SIGN OF HIM -

WELL-I'M TIRED OF LOOKING-MOTHER-MAYBE FATHER WENT BACK TO THE HOTEL-
HE WOULDN'T DO ANYTHING AS SENSIBLE AS THAT-DID YOU GO IN THE TREASURY BUILDING TO LOOK FOR HIM?
YES-AND THE FEDERAL BUREAU OF INVESTIGATION-MR. JOHN EDGAR HOOVER-WHO IS A FRIEND OF YOUR HUSBAND-WILL TRY TO FIND HIM-

DO YOU THINK HE MET SOME SENATOR HE KNOWS AND WENT TO LUNCH OR SOMETHING?
HERE I AM TRYING TO FIND HIM AND YOU TALK OF MIRACLES-
WELL-COME ON-WE'LL NOT FIND HIM STANDING HERE-

MOTHER-I'M ALL IN FROM WALKING-LET'S GO BACK TO THE HOTEL-WE CAN'T FIND HIM-
IF HE'S WITHIN A MILE OF HERE-I'M GOING TO FIND HIM-BOTH OF YOU WAIT RIGHT HERE-
I'D JOLLY WELL LIKE TO SIT DOWN-
Copr. 1940, King Features Syndicate, Inc., World rights reserved

JIGGS!
3-17

JIGGS!
GEO McMANUS

AREN'T THESE WONDERFUL PICTURES OF OUR TRIP? LOOK AT THIS ONE TAKEN IN ST LOUIS-

BY JOVE-I'M GLAD I SAW THIS PHOTO OF ME IN TOLEDO - I DO NOT REMEMBER BEING THERE-

BY GOLLY-HERE IS ONE OF US IN KANSAS CITY-SOME TOWN-

HERE IS ONE OF US AT MRS. SIPALOT'S TEA PARTY IN BOSTON-

Picture taken in the desert Papa is in the center of the totem-poles - He went on the water wagon for two weeks

Our beautiful trip up the Mississippi river - We landed where the Missouri river runs into the Mississippi and Jiggs ran into Dinty Moore, Mother angry as usual.

This was taken just after daddy met President Roosevelt, Two buttons flew off his vest. Mother is jealous but happy -

Atlantic City, N.J. Attracted a lot of attention - all well and happy.

San Francisco Chinatown, Mother had a fine time, Father was with her.

GEO MCMANUS

Albuquerque, Father and son-in-law - We are still packing blankets - arrows - Indian relics, etc. that they bought. Maggie still angry.

Picture of Maggie's cousin, "Wacky" in his mansion near Weehawken, N.J. He is taking life easy, and it looks as if it won't last long.

Picture taken in a New York night club, Negative was destroyed, Father was nearly destroyed by mother

3-24

LOOK AT THE FUNNY HATS WE WORE LAST NIGHT AT JERRY'S BEEFSTEAK- WOW- DID WE HAVE FUN!
HA- HA-
TRY IT ON-JUST THINK, THE DINNER AND ALL THE TRIMMINGS COST ONLY TWO BUCKS-
GEE-DIDN'T THE FUNNY HAT COST ANYTHING?
MANY REQUESTS FOR JIGGS' FAMOUS CORNED BEEF AND CABBAGE RECIPE HAVE BEEN RECEIVED-
WE'LL GLADLY MAIL IT TO YOU IF YOU SEND IN A SELF-ADDRESSED-STAMPED ENVELOPE TO-
GEORGE McMANUS
THE HAT IS PAPER GEE-YOU LOOK FUNNY WITH IT ON-GOSH, THAT CERTAINLY IS A COMICAL HAT-
DO I LOOK AS FUNNY AS YOU WITH IT ON?
HELLO-ARCHIE DARLING-I JUST DROPPED IN TO SHOW YOU MY NEW HAT-IT IS AN EXCLUSIVE STYLE-ISN'T IT BEAUTIFUL?
HUH-OH-YES- IS THAT THE LATEST STYLE FOR WOMEN?
3-31
Copr. 1940, King Features Syndicate, Inc., World rights reserved.
BE SURE YOU GET THE BUNKER HILL MONUMENT IN THE PICTURES, AS IT IS ONE OF THE MOST HISTORICAL SPOTS IN BOSTON-
KEEP MOVING- REMEMBER- THIS IS A MOVING PICTURE CAMERA-
HOW DARE YOU?
AND YOU KEEP MOVING-CAN'T YOU READ THE SIGNS THAT SAY- "KEEP OFF THE GRASS"?
DO YOU THINK YOU'RE TH' BOSS OF BOSTON?
WE'LL GET THAT PICTURE LATER- THERE IS THE OLD NORTH CHURCH-IT'S HISTORICAL-TAKE A PICTURE OF IT-
HOW KIN I-WITH ALL OF THEM TRUCKS AND CARS IN THE WAY? LET'S GO TO TH' PUBLIC GARDEN-
VAN
I'M SORRY-LADY- BUT AS YOU SEE- IT'S NO USE TAKIN' A PICTURE OF THAT STATUE-WHY DON'T YOU GO UP TO 19 NORTH SQUARE? IT IS PAUL REVERE'S HOUSE-
YOU SHOULD HAVE WAITED AND TAKEN A PICTURE OF THE OLD STATE HOUSE- IT IS VERY HISTORICAL-
DON'T BOTHER ME NOW-I WANT TO GIT A PICTURE OF OLD IRONSIDES!
TAKE A PICTURE OF THE DOORWAY INTO PAUL REVERE'S HOUSE-
HOW CAN I WITH THOSE GUYS STANDING IN FRONT OF IT? LETS GO ELSEWHERE-
BEN AND SAM'S SUITS
HAT SALE AT NITA'S
DUNK DO-NUTS AT DUGAN'S DINER
BY GOLLY-THERE'S TH' OLD STATE HOUSE- I'LL SEE IF I KIN GET A PICTURE OF IT--
DON'T TAKE IT UNTIL THAT WINDOW WASHER GETS OUT OF THE WAY-
WELL-WHY DIDN'T YOU TAKE IT WHEN YOU HAD A CHANCE?
HOW DID I KNOW THAT BOAT WUZ GONNA PARK IN FRONT OF IT?
LOOK-QUICK! TAKE A PICTURE OF THAT AIRPLANE LANDING IN THE WATER-
THE STARTER- OR WHATEVER YOU CALL IT- IS STUCK-
I'M THROUGH!
GEO McMANUS
Copr. 1940, King Features Syndicate, Inc., World rights reserved
3-31
OH-WE GOT SOME BEAUTIFUL POST-CARDS OF BOSTON- HERE'S ONE OF THE CONCORD BRIDGE-
HERE'S A NICE ONE OF FANEUIL HALL-
THIS IS ONE OF THE OLD STATE HOUSE-
IF I HAD ONLY GOTTEN A PICTURE OF ONE SCENE- I'D HAVE BEEN SATISFIED-

GEE-ROSIE-THE BOSS BAWLED ME OUT-HE SAID I HAD A MIND LIKE AN ANT-THAT I COULDN'T REMEMBER ANYTHING-
I THINK HE IS JUST HORRID-THE ANSWER IS YOU'RE TOO INTELLIGENT FOR THAT JOB-

YOU DARLING-YOU MAKE ME HAPPY-THIS WORLD WOULD BE NOTHING WITHOUT YOU-
NOW-YOU STOP WORRYING-I WANT YOU TO GO TO THE STORE FOR ME-AS I AM GOING TO FIX A NICE DINNER FOR YOU-

GET A LOAF OF BREAD-SOME POTATOES-A BOTTLE OF MILK AND SOME COFFEE-I'LL HAVE EVERYTHING READY WHEN YOU GET BACK-
ALL RIGHT-DEARIE-I WON'T BE LONG-
4-7

ROSIE IS RIGHT-I'M WASTING MY TIME AT THAT OFFICE-I SHOULD BE AN EXECUTIVE-
Copr. 1940, King Features Syndicate, Inc., World rights reserved

ROSIE-I'M AT THE STORE NOW-WHAT DID YOU TELL ME TO GET?

I'M SORRY-SIR-BUT YOUR WIFE SAID THERE WERE SIX GRIPS-BUT THERE WERE ONLY FIVE IN THE AUTO YOU FOLKS ARRIVED IN-
YOU MUST THINK THAT I KNOW EVERYTHING-HOW WOULD I KNOW HOW MANY THERE WERE?

WURRA-WURRA-NO ONE DOES ANYTHING RIGHT IN THIS FAMILY BUT ME-IF IT WASN'T FOR ME-WE WOULDN'T BE IN BALTIMORE NOW!

WHAT'S THE MATTER?
I LEFT MY PURSE IN THE LAST TOWN WE STOPPED IN FOR LUNCH-I MUST FIND OUT THE NAME OF IT-

BY JOVE-I JUST HAPPENED TO THINK-DID I GIVE YOU THE KEYS TO MY GRIP? AND IF SO-WHERE IS MY GRIP?
I KNEW SOMETHING WOULD HAPPEN IF YOU STARTED TO THINK-

NOW-WHAT DO YOU WANT?
SORRY-OLD BOZO-MY ERROR-I THOUGHT THIS WUZ ROOM 206-BUT IF THERE'S A PIPE LEAKIN' IN HERE-I'D JUST AS SOON FIX IT-

DID YOU REMEMBER TO BRING FIFI'S DOGGIE BISCUITS? AND DID I ASK YOU TO REMIND ME OF ANYTHING?
YES-YES-I'VE TAKEN CARE OF EVERYTHING BUT MYSELF-

IF IT WUZN'T FOR ME-THIS FAMILY WOULD NEVER GET ANYWHERE-
DAUGHTER-HAVE YOU WRITTEN SONNY THAT LETTER?

I JUST REMEMBERED-I DIDN'T PUT MY BLUE SLIPPERS IN MY GRIP-I LEFT THEM IN THE LAST TOWN-
I PUT THEM IN MY SUIT-CASE-SO STOP WORRYING-

NOW WHAT AILS YOU AGAIN? BY GOLLY-I HAVE TO DO EVERYTHING AROUND HERE-
I'M SORRY-BUT DID I ASK YOU IF YOU HAD MY KEYS TO MY GRIP OR DID I TELL YOU I HAD THEM?

DADDY-WHERE ARE MY-
NOW-LISTEN-I'M TIRED OF ANSWERING QUESTIONS-WE'D NEVER GIT ANYWHERE IF IT WASN'T FER ME-I'M GOING OUT AND FIND OUT SOMETHING ABOUT BALTIMORE-

WHAT'S THAT?
OFFICER-IS THERE A BUREAU OF INFORMATION HERE IN BALTIMORE?
Copr. 1940, King Features Syndicate, Inc., World rights reserved.
4-7

BALTIMORE? THIS ISN'T BALTIMORE-THIS IS THE CITY OF TRENTON, NEW JERSEY-
?

GEE-I HOPE ROSIE WON'T BE ANGRY AT ME BECAUSE I FORGOT AND HAD TO 'PHONE TO ASK HER WHAT SHE TOLD ME TO GET AT THE STORE-
AH-YOU FORGIVE ME-YOU DEAR-I HOPE YOU DON'T THINK I HAVE NO MEMORY-
CERTAINLY-LOVEY-ANYONE IS APT TO FORGET ONCE IN A WHILE-NOW LET ME HELP YOU-JUST SIT DOWN WHILE I FIX THE DINNER-DEAR-
GEE-THE BOSS THINKS I AM A "FOR-RENT HEAD"-BUT ROSIE KNOWS BETTER-
WHY-DARLING-YOU FORGOT THE BREAD AND POTATOES AND THE CHOPS-OH-DEAR-YOU DIDN'T BRING THE BUTTER--
DID I-DEAR? I GUESS I FORGOT-
Copr. 1940, King Features Syndicate, Inc., World rights reserved.
ARCHIE-DEAR-WHAT IN THE WORLD DID YOU BRING THAT BOX OF BIRD SEED FOR?
?
4-14

GEE-JIGGS-IT MUST BE WONDERFUL TO TRAVEL ALL OVER THE COUNTRY-HOW DO YOU LIKE IT HERE IN CLEVELAND?
IT'S A GRAND CITY-BUT YOU'RE NO HELP TO IT-BY GOLLY-I'M MOVIN' SO MUCH-I THINK I WILL SLEEP IN AN ELEVATOR SO THERE WON'T BE ANY STOPS IN ME TRAVELING-
THAT'S ODD-RUNNIN' INTO BEN LOFFIN-ESPECIALLY IN CLEVELAND-AND OUT OF JAIL-WELL-I MUST GET HOME AN' FIND OUT WHAT WE ARE TO DO NEXT-
A FUNNY THING HAPPENED-YOUR LAWYER BACK HOME JUST 'PHONED AND SAID YOU LOST THAT CASE IN COURT-AND YOU FORGOT TO MAKE OUT YOUR INCOME TAX-
NOW-AIN'T THAT FUNNY? THAT ADDS TO THIS TRIP A LOT-
FATHER-OUR CHAUFFEUR WAS JUST HERE AND SAYS, THAT WE NEED ALL NEW TIRES ON THE CAR-IT ALSO NEEDS OVERHAULING-
THAT GUY MAKES ME TIRED-I'M THE ONE THAT'S BEING OVER-HAULED-
I'M SORRY-BUT THESE TICKETS FROM CLEVELAND TO LOUISVILLE ARE NOT GOOD BY THE WAY OF AKRON-YOU'LL HAVE TO GO TO NEW YORK BY THE WAY OF BOSTON-THEN TO ERIE AND ON TO NIAGARA FALLS-
NO WONDER-ME WIFE HAD HER BROTHER GIT THOSE TICKETS-HE'S MAD ABOUT CROSS-WORD PUZZLES-
BUT-MAGGIE-I'VE GOT EVERYTHING PACKED-
I DON'T CARE-YOU GOT TO GET THAT CAPE OUT-YOU'VE PACKED IT SOMEWHERE-

BY GOLLY-I CAN'T FIND HER CAPE-I'VE EVERYTHING OUT OF TH' GRIPS-
SHE SAYS-NEVER MIND-SHE JUST REMEMBERED SHE DIDN'T BRING IT-
I WANT YOU TO CALL UP SONNY AND SEE HOW HE IS-I KNOW THE POOR BOY IS LONESOME-
WELL-WHAT'S THE USE OF CALLIN' HIM UP IF YOU KNOW IT?
OH-IT'S TOO DIFFICULT TO FIGURE OUT-DEAR-LET DADDY DO IT-AS WE MUST SEE MORE OF CLEVELAND BEFORE WE LEAVE-
YES-AND BESIDES-WE WON'T HAVE TO GET INTO ANY ARGUMENT WITH YOUR MOTHER ABOUT IT-

AN' ME EITHER-
Copr. 1940, King Features Syndicate, Inc., World rights reserved.

I WOULD GIVE A FORTUNE RIGHT NOW JUST TO BE TURNING THE KNOB ON DINTY'S FRONT DOOR-
HELLO-JIGGS-IT MUST BE GREAT TO TRAVEL ALL AROUND THE COUNTRY WITH YOUR FAMILY-TAKIN' LIFE EASY-JUST A CARE-FREE BOY-
4-14

GEO McMANUS
NOW-LISTEN-THIS IS NO PLACE TO START A FIGHT-
I'M NOT GOIN' TO START-I'M GOIN' TO FINISH IT-

ARCHIE DARLING - I'M GOING OVER TO AUNT SUSIE'S AND I WANT YOU TO MEET ME AT HER HOUSE - NOW DO NOT DISAPPOINT ME - HERE'S THE ADDRESS - WRITE IT DOWN - NOW - DEAREST DON'T FAIL TO BE THERE -
I WON'T - LOVEY - I'LL BE THERE JUST AS SOON AS I FINISH WORK - I HAVE THE ADDRESS WRITTEN DOWN - SWEETIE - SEE YOU SOON -
I NEVER MET HER AUNT - BUT I WILL BET SHE HAS A SWELL DINNER - GOSH - IT'S SWELL - IT'S NEARLY FIVE O'CLOCK -
Copr. 1940, King Features Syndicate, Inc., World rights reserved.
NOW - WHERE IS THAT ADDRESS - I AM POSITIVE I LEFT IT RIGHT HERE ON MY DESK -
4-21
WHERE IN THE WORLD DID IT GO? I THOUGHT SURE I'D HAVE IT IF I WROTE IT DOWN - I CAN'T FIND IT -
MR. AND MRS. PHILIP ATMEALS HAVE INVITED US TO DINE WITH THEM TONIGHT - IT IS TO BE ONE OF THE BIGGEST SOCIAL AFFAIRS OF THE YEAR IN CHICAGO -
BUT - MOTHER - I CAN'T GO - YOU KNOW I AM ON A DIET - I'D FEEL OUT OF PLACE -
AND I HAVE SUCH A COLD I COULDN'T EAT A BITE -
I WISH I COULD THINK UP AN EXCUSE AS FAST AS THAT - I'M STUCK -
ISN'T IT TOO BAD OUR CHILDREN COULDN'T COME? THEIR CUISINE IS NOTED IN SOCIAL CIRCLES ALL OVER THE COUNTRY -
I NEVER MET HER COUSIN - BUT YER COUSIN "BIMMY" IS KNOWN ALL OVER THE COUNTRY -
T-42
JOHN - DON'T EAT THOSE POTATOES - REMEMBER WHAT DR. DICKEY SAID ABOUT YOUR HEART -
NO - I NEVER EAT IN THE EVENING - BESIDES, I'M ON A DIET AND SO SICK IT'S DELIGHTFUL -
WOULD YOU MIND TAKING THAT SOUP AWAY? IT CONTAINS TOO MANY CALORIES -
PAUL - YOU'VE HAD TWO OLIVES - I KNOW YOU WILL BE SICK -
JUST BRING ME A DRINK OF HOT WATER - THAT'S ALL -
I JUST HAD A TOOTH PULLED - AND CAN'T EAT A THING -
I'VE ALWAYS BEEN SUCH A LIGHT EATER - MY TASTE IS SO DELICATE -
NO, THANKS - I MUSTN'T EAT ANY SQUAB - I KNOW I'LL BE CALLED ON TO SING AND EATING IMPAIRS MY VOICE - SO -
GRACIOUS - I SHOULDN'T HAVE EATEN THAT PECAN - NOW I'VE GOT INDIGESTION -
MARIE - I CAN'T EAT - I FORGOT MY PILLS -
I JUST CAN'T EAT TONIGHT AS I'VE HAD MY QUOTA OF VITAMINS -
I'M SORRY I CAN'T EAT THAT - IT HAS SALT IN IT -
I CAN'T EAT RADISHES WITH CARROTS - SO I WON'T EAT EITHER -
I'D LOVE TO EAT A COOKIE - BUT THEY DON'T AGREE WITH ME -
ELMER - PUT DOWN THAT BUN -
IF I WASN'T SO BILIOUS I'D ENJOY EATING -
MAGGIE, KIN I?
DEAR - YOU SHOULD HAVE BEEN THERE - SUCH FOOD AND MY - THE SERVICE - I NEVER SAW SO MUCH FOOD - SUCH A PLENTY - EVERYTHING ONE COULD DESIRE - MY - THE MOST DELICIOUS COOKING - EVERYTHING YOU COULD THINK OF -
SIT DOWN, MOTHER - TELL ME ALL ABOUT IT -
WELL - I'M NOT GOIN' TO LISTEN TO WHAT I COULD HAVE EATEN IF THEY WOULD HAVE LET ME -
Copr. 1940, King Features Syndicate, Inc., World rights reserved.
YEAH - ANOTHER PLATE OF BEANS, SOME OYSTERS AN' MORE BUNS AND POTATOES - A SIDE ORDER OF GOULASH AN' SOME HAM -
BOY - YOU ORDER AS IF YOU HAVEN'T EATEN ALL DAY -
A CUP OF JAVA - JERRY -
JERRY, GIMME ANOTHER SLAB OF BEEF -
DISH UP SOME MORE BEANS -
4-21

I'M GLAD THE PARTY THAT ROSIE AND I ARE GOING TO IS ONLY FIVE BLOCKS FROM HER HOUSE- AS I CAN'T AFFORD A TAXI -

WELL-ARE YOU READY-ROSIE? IT'LL BE A NICE LITTLE WALK OVER TO THE PARTY-BUT-OF COURSE-IF YOU WISH TO RIDE-

OH-I THINK THAT WILL BE FINE-JUST A MINUTE-UNTIL I GET MY COAT-

OH-DEAR-IT'S STARTING TO RAIN-NOW WE WILL HAVE TO TAKE A TAXI--

JUST A MINUTE-DARLING-I HEAR MY 'PHONE-I'LL BE RIGHT BACK-

HUH?

OH-YES-AUNT SUSIE-WHY-CERTAINLY NOT-ARCHIE AND I WILL BE DELIGHTED TO CALL FOR YOU-WHY-YOUR HOUSE IS ONLY ABOUT A MILE OUT OF OUR WAY-WE DON'T MIND-DEAR -

4-28

1

MRS AL TOONA HAS INVITED ME TO VISIT HER-AS SHE AND MRS HARRIS BURG WANT TO MAKE PLANS TO TAKE US SIGHT-SEEING HERE IN PITTSBURGH-I'LL BE BACK LATER-I WISH YOU WOULD READ A BOOK AND ELEVATE YOURSELF WHILE I AM AWAY-

DON'T WORRY-I'LL ELEVATE MESELF ALL RIGHT-

2

AH! MRS AL TOONA-MY-WHAT A BEAUTIFUL APARTMENT YOU HAVE HERE IN PITTSBURGH-HOW DID YOU FIND OUT I WAS IN TOWN?

OH-BY THE SOCIETY COLUMN-OF COURSE-NOW, FIRST I MUST SHOW YOU MY APARTMENT-I HOPE YOU DON'T MIND THAT NOISE-AS THEY ARE ERECTING A NEW BUILDING NEXT DOOR-

3

IT'S GOOD TO SEE YOU-JIGGS-YOUR OLD PAL-DUGAN-IS COMING DOWN TO TAKE YOU UP TO SEE TH' VIEW-

DINTY TOLD ME I'D FIND YOU HERE-THERE'S DUGAN NOW-A GRAND GUY-HE IS ALWAYS ON THE JOB-

4

YEP-JIGGS-WHEN I LEFT THE OLD TOWN I CAME HERE TO PITTSBURGH-AND I HAVEN'T BEEN OUT OF WORK ONE DAY-IT'S A GREAT CITY-

BY GOLLY-WE'RE SO HIGH NOW-WE'RE OUT OF TOWN-

7

BUT-MRS. JIGGS-I WANT YOU TO STAY FOR DINNER-WE HAVEN'T LAID ANY PLANS FOR OUR TRIP TOMORROW-

SORRY-BUT I'VE SOMETHING TO ATTEND TO RIGHT AWAY-

LOOK-FELLOWS-JERRY'S SWEETIE GOT HIM THAT TIE AND SHE MAKES HIM WEAR IT-IF SHE CARED FOR YOU-SHE WOULDN'T MAKE YOU WEAR IT-
HAVE TO WEAR IT-EH?
HE WOULDN'T IF HE DIDN'T HAVE TO-
GEE-FELLOWS-CUT OUT THE KIDDING-SHE THINKS IT IS BEAUTIFUL-I DON'T WANT TO OFFEND HER-SO I WEAR IT-
YOU LOOK AS IF YOUR CHEST IS ON FIRE-
THAT TIE LOOKS LIKE A WRECKED PAINT SHOP-I WOULDN'T WEAR IT TO A DOG FIGHT-
Copr. 1940, King Features Syndicate, Inc., World rights reserved.
LOOK-ARCHIE-DARLING-I SAW THIS TIE IN A WINDOW-IT'S LOVELY-SO I GOT IT FOR YOU-PUT IT ON RIGHT NOW BEFORE YOU GO BACK TO YOUR OFFICE-I'LL TAKE THE ONE YOU HAVE ON-
YOU WANT ME TO WEAR IT NOW?
5-5
HELLO-SAY-TIM-I WON'T BE BACK TO THE OFFICE TODAY-I DON'T FEEL WELL-
JUST THINK-HERE WE ARE IN ATLANTIC CITY-BUT WE MUST UNPACK EVERYTHING BEFORE WE TAKE A STROLL ON THE BOARD WALK-
HOW SILLY OF ME-WHEN I HEARD PEOPLE SPEAK OF THE PIERS HERE-I THOUGHT THEY WERE TALKING OF THE NOBILITY-
MAGGIE-I THINK I'LL TAKE A STROLL-IS IT O-KAY WITH YOU?
IT'S ALL RIGHT WITH ME IF YOU TAKE A STROLL AND IT WOULD BE WONDERFUL IF YOU COULD THINK-
OH-BOY-THIS SEA-AIR CERTAINLY IS GREAT-I THINK I'LL STROLL DOWN TO TH' RAILROAD TRACK-I MIGHT FIND SOMEONE THAT I KNOW-
BY GOLLY-I HAVEN'T BEEN IN THE OCEAN FOR A DIP IN TWENTY YEARS-BUT I'M GOIN' IN NOW-
BUT LET ME EXPLAIN-DEAR-I WAS JUST STUDYIN' THE STYLES-
HERE'S A SNAPPY SUIT-THAT WILL JUST FIT YOU-BEAUTIFUL DAY-ISN'T IT?
EVERYTHING'S BEAUTIFUL-
?
OH-I JUST CAN'T RESIST-I MUST PUT ON MY NEW BATHING-SUIT-
GEO McMANUS
Copr. 1940, King Features Syndicate, Inc., World rights reserved.
5-5

Copr. 1940, King Features Syndicate, Inc., World rights reserved

Maggie, do you remember when...

WHAT IN THE WORLD ARE YOU LAUGHING AT? WHAT HAVE YOU GOT THERE?

I WUZ RUMMAGIN' AROUND IN THE ATTIC AN' FOUND THIS OLD PICTURE ALBUM-IT HAS PICTURES OF YOU AN' ALL YOUR RELATIONS-

Picture of Maggie, taken in front of Washentear Laundry where she worked 1903.

Our daughter-Nora on way to Caseys brick-yard with daddy's dinner

Aug 6 1913.

Maggie with mamma and papa at Coney Island-June 9. 1888.

Picture taken in front of house on Dill Street near the Gas-house-Mimmie sitting in the door way-Larry was just six when he had his first fight.

←Rover-The best ratter in town.

Maggie and Larry at play.

Sunday May 1, 1904

Jiggs and Maggie in turn-out loaned by our grocer.

Maggie's brother Larry on way to work.

When he was working.

Cousin Dinny and Betsy of the Cass Ave Line

×is Betsy.

Jan. 3. 1911. Jiggs leads Maggie to the preacher-That ended his leadership.

Maggie at the age of six

July 6. 1894.

Taken in the alley

Saturday night at Cousin Kate's house.

Jiggs and Maggie at the Ash-wagon drivers' picnic.

April 7. 1909-

GREAT HEAVENS-BURN THAT BOOK IMMEDIATELY-

HERE'S A PICTURE OF YOUR BROTHER-LARRY-BEFORE HE WENT TO JAIL-

Maggie and Clancy's son-Hector-in O'Fallen Park.

I LOVE MAGGIE

Aunt Agnes and Mike her beau. Maggie in the middle

Cousin Jim

GEO McMANUS

2-5

WHAT IN THE WORLD IS ON YOUR MIND?

AH-MAGGIE-ME DARLIN', I WUZ JUST DREAMIN' ABOUT THE OLD DAYS-THE GOOD TIMES WE HAD-REMEMBER—

WHEN YOU USE' TO DANCE ON THE SIDEWALK TO THE GOOD OLD TUNE OF "TWO LITTLE GIRLS IN BLUE"

AN' HOW SHY YOU WUZ THE DAY I PROPOSED TO YOU ON THE BOAT GOIN' TO CONEY ISLAND-YOU WUZ WORKIN' IN THE RIPENTEAR LAUNDRY-

AN' WHEN MARY O'BRIEN CAME HOME FROM NEW YORK WITH THAT NEW FANG-DANGLED KANGAROO WALK

SHE WAS HAPPY TILL SHE MET YOU AND THE FAULT IS ALL YOUR OWN

AN' THE OLD GANG WOULD GIT TOGETHER AT YOUR HOUSE ON SATURDAY NIGHT AN' SING ALL THE OLD TUNES-THEY WUZ KNOWN AS "THE ALLEY-CATS QUARTETTE"

CIGARS

AN' I'D MEET YOU ON THE WAY TO THE STORE AN' I'D CARRY YOUR BASKET AN LET YOU CARRY THE BUCKET-

AN' HOW STUCK-UP DINNY DUGAN WUZ WHEN HE WUZ RIDIN' ON HIS HIGH WHEEL BICYCLE-

AN' THE DAY YOUR BROTHER LARRY WORE HIS FIRST PAIR OF LONG PANTS-

AN' THE HAPPY DAYS WE SPENT GOIN' DOWN THE BAY ON CLANCY'S CHOWDER PARTIES AN' THE BAR WUZ ON THE LEFT HAND SIDE OF THE BOAT AN' HOW IT USED TO TIP ON ACCOUNT OF THAT-

THERE IT IS, MAGGIE-

NOW AIN'T THAT JUST GRAND?

LEMME SEE-MA-MA-

AN' THE DAY I GOT ME FIRST RAISE WORKIN' IN FINNIGAN'S BRICK YARD AN' HOW I COULD EAT EIGHT OR NINE HELPIN'S OF CORNED BEEF AN' HOW OUR BEAUTIFUL LITTLE DAUGHTER LIKED PIG'S KNUCKLES-

WEREN'T WE HAPPY-DARLING? I WISH WE COULD LIVE THOSE DAYS ALL OVER AGAIN

AH-MAGGIE-THEM DAYS IS GONE FOREVER-DO YOU REMEMBER LITTLE "RED HEAD" DANNY?

4-30

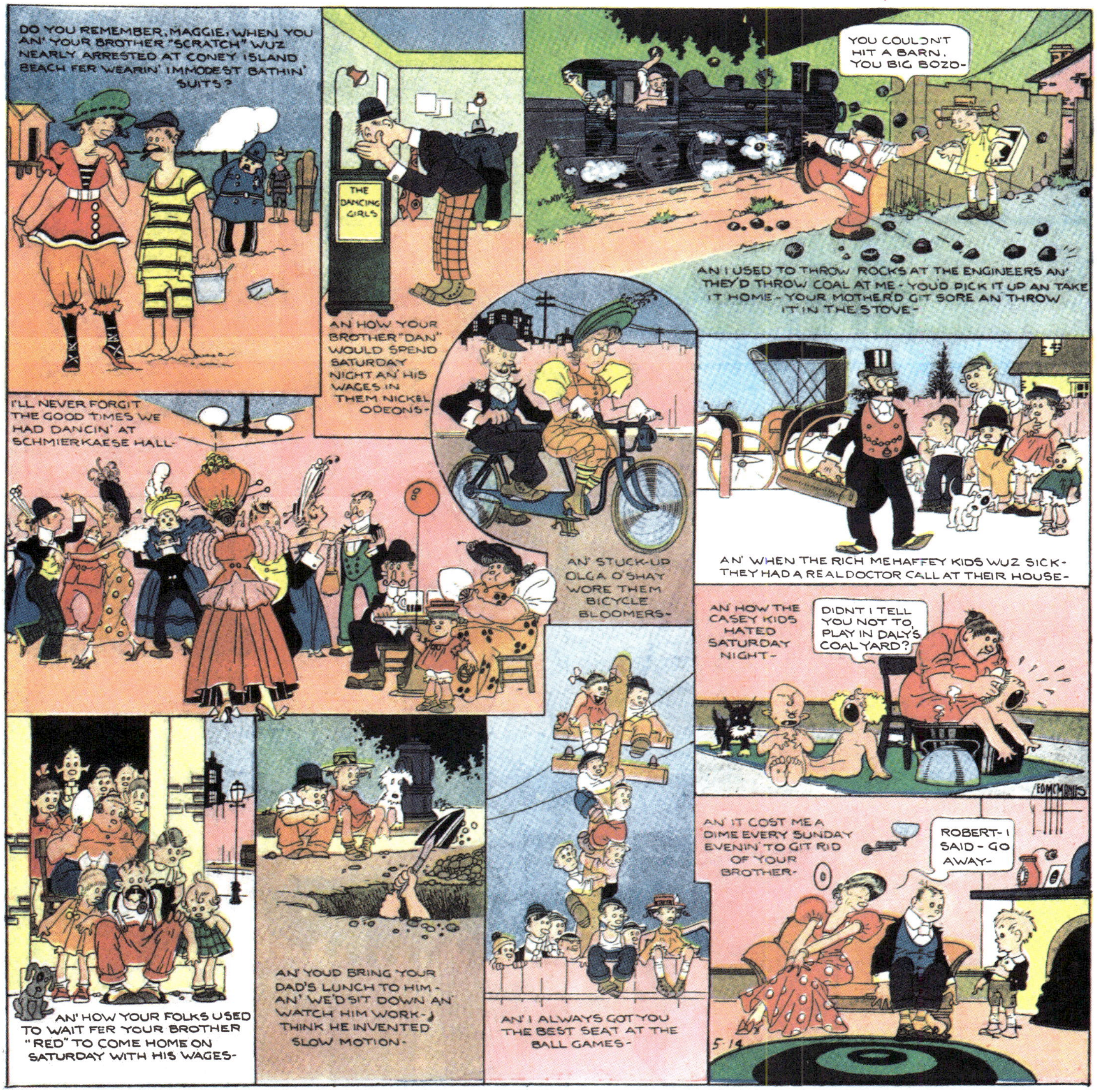

DO YOU REMEMBER, MAGGIE, WHEN YOU AN' YOUR BROTHER "SCRATCH" WUZ NEARLY ARRESTED AT CONEY ISLAND BEACH FER WEARIN' IMMODEST BATHIN' SUITS?

THE DANCING GIRLS

AN' HOW YOUR BROTHER "DAN" WOULD SPEND SATURDAY NIGHT AN' HIS WAGES IN THEM NICKEL ODEONS-

YOU COULDN'T HIT A BARN, YOU BIG BOZO-

AN' I USED TO THROW ROCKS AT THE ENGINEERS AN' THEY'D THROW COAL AT ME-YOU'D PICK IT UP AN TAKE IT HOME-YOUR MOTHER'D GIT SORE AN THROW IT IN THE STOVE-

I'LL NEVER FORGIT THE GOOD TIMES WE HAD DANCIN' AT SCHMIERKAESE HALL-

AN' STUCK-UP OLGA O'SHAY WORE THEM BICYCLE BLOOMERS-

AN' WHEN THE RICH MEHAFFEY KIDS WUZ SICK-THEY HAD A REAL DOCTOR CALL AT THEIR HOUSE-

AN' HOW THE CASEY KIDS HATED SATURDAY NIGHT-

DIDN'T I TELL YOU NOT TO PLAY IN DALY'S COAL YARD?

EDMCMANUS

AN' HOW YOUR FOLKS USED TO WAIT FER YOUR BROTHER "RED" TO COME HOME ON SATURDAY WITH HIS WAGES-

AN' YOU'D BRING YOUR DAD'S LUNCH TO HIM-AN' WE'D SIT DOWN AN' WATCH HIM WORK-THINK HE INVENTED SLOW MOTION-

AN' I ALWAYS GOT YOU THE BEST SEAT AT THE BALL GAMES-

AN' IT COST ME A DIME EVERY SUNDAY EVENIN' TO GIT RID OF YOUR BROTHER-

ROBERT-I SAID-GO AWAY-

5-14

GEE' I HAVENT EVEN A DIME CAR-FARE TO GET ME TO ROSIE'S HOUSE AND SHE'S EXPECTING ME TO CALL THIS EVENING -
EVEN IF I STARTED, TO WALK I WOULDNT GET THERE UNTIL MIDNIGHT- IF I COULD ONLY THINK OF A WAY?
THIS IS STATION C-O-D-
THINGS WE CAN DO WITHOUT--
?
IF YOU NEED MONEY- WE LEND ON ANY-THING AND EVERY-THING- CLOCKS- WATCHES - LAMPS-
BY GOLLY' THE RADIO EVEN THINKS FOR YOU-
PAWN SHOP

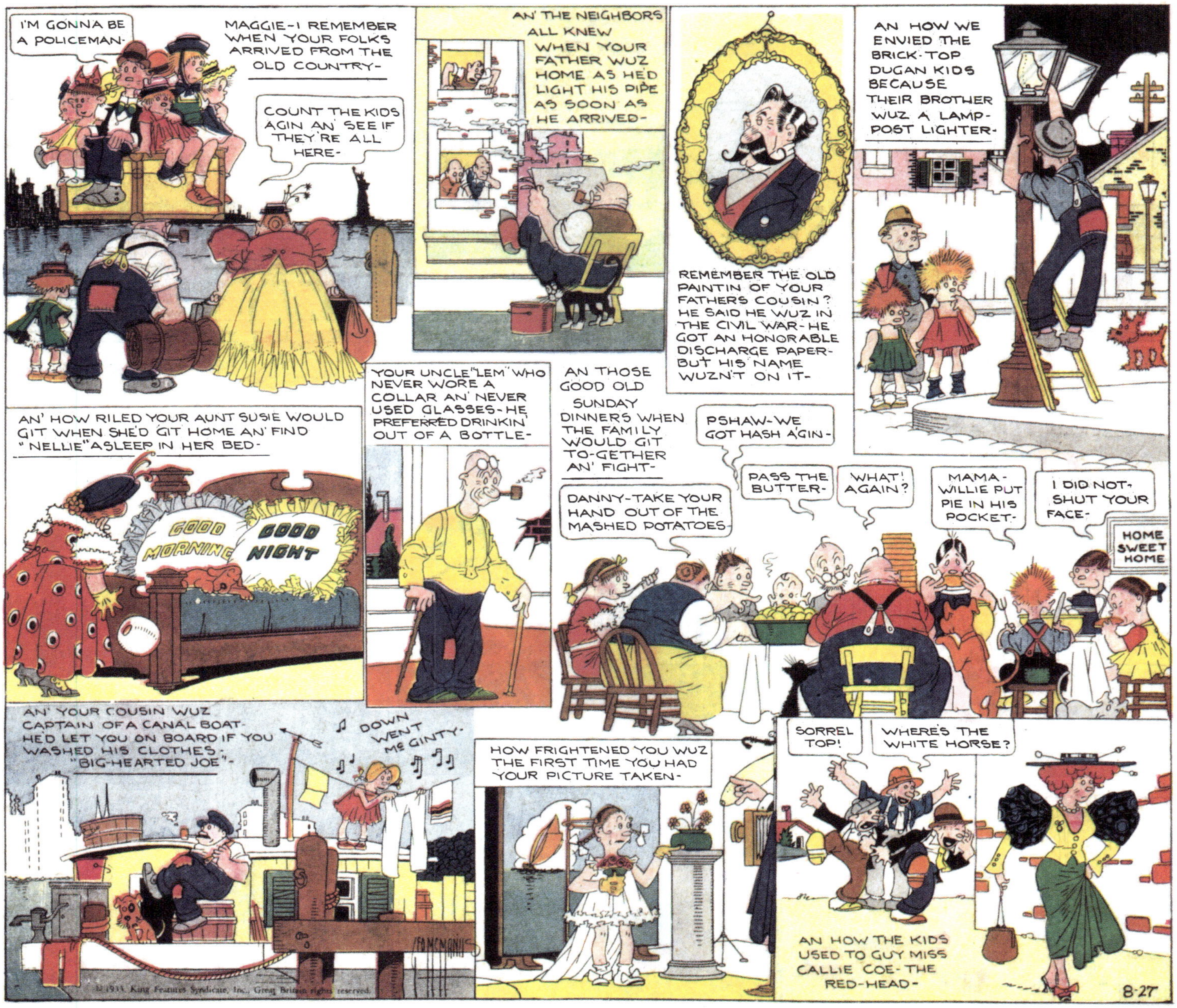

I'M GONNA BE A POLICEMAN-
MAGGIE-I REMEMBER WHEN YOUR FOLKS ARRIVED FROM THE OLD COUNTRY-
COUNT THE KIDS AGIN AN' SEE IF THEY'RE ALL HERE-
AN' THE NEIGHBORS ALL KNEW WHEN YOUR FATHER WUZ HOME AS HE'D LIGHT HIS PIPE AS SOON AS HE ARRIVED-
REMEMBER THE OLD PAINTIN OF YOUR FATHERS COUSIN? HE SAID HE WUZ IN THE CIVIL WAR- HE GOT AN HONORABLE DISCHARGE PAPER- BUT HIS NAME WUZN'T ON IT-
AN HOW WE ENVIED THE BRICK-TOP DUGAN KIDS BECAUSE THEIR BROTHER WUZ A LAMP-POST LIGHTER-
AN' HOW RILED YOUR AUNT SUSIE WOULD GIT WHEN SHE'D GIT HOME AN' FIND "NELLIE" ASLEEP IN HER BED-
GOOD MORNING
GOOD NIGHT
YOUR UNCLE "LEM" WHO NEVER WORE A COLLAR AN' NEVER USED GLASSES- HE PREFERRED DRINKIN' OUT OF A BOTTLE-
AN THOSE GOOD OLD SUNDAY DINNERS WHEN THE FAMILY WOULD GIT TO-GETHER AN' FIGHT-
PSHAW-WE GOT HASH AGIN-
PASS THE BUTTER-
WHAT! AGAIN?
MAMA - WILLIE PUT PIE IN HIS POCKET-
I DID NOT- SHUT YOUR FACE-
DANNY-TAKE YOUR HAND OUT OF THE MASHED POTATOES-
HOME SWEET HOME
AN' YOUR COUSIN WUZ CAPTAIN OF A CANAL BOAT- HE'D LET YOU ON BOARD IF YOU WASHED HIS CLOTHES- "BIG-HEARTED JOE"-
DOWN WENT MC GINTY-
HOW FRIGHTENED YOU WUZ THE FIRST TIME YOU HAD YOUR PICTURE TAKEN-
SORREL TOP!
WHERE'S THE WHITE HORSE?
AN HOW THE KIDS USED TO GUY MISS CALLIE COE- THE RED-HEAD-
McMANUS
8-27

REMEMBER THE DAYS WHEN THE BACK-YARD GOSSIP WAS ALL THE VOGUE?

DID YOU SEE THE CONDITION HER HUSBAND CAME HOME IN LAST NIGHT?

AN HER SON IS JUST A "GOOD-FER-NOTHIN'"-

THE PATROL WAGON HAS BEEN THERE TWICE THIS WEEK-

THE DAUGHTER USES FACE POWDER-

AN', MAGGIE! REMEMBER WHEN YOUR BROTHER DANNY GOT A JOB AS ENGINEER AN' WE ALL WAITED AT THE STATION TO SEE HIM BRING THE TRAIN IN-

SHE WAS HAPPY UNTIL SHE MET YOU----

HOLD IT.

BREAD

THE OLD AWNIN' QUARTETTE-

AN' THE DAY I WENT UP THE POLE AN' GOT YOUR KITE-

AN' THE PICTURE YOU HAD TAKEN ON OUR WEDDIN' DAY- THE SAME DAY YOUR UNCLE GOT OUT OF JAIL AN' YOUR COUSIN WENT IN-

THE BARBER SHOP WHERE GUSTAVE PRETZELHAUF-THE BUTCHER, HAD A SHAVIN'-CUP WITH HIS NAME ON IT- AN' ALL THE LIVER HE USED TO GIVE US FER THE CAT-

HOW'S BUSINESS, JOE?

ALL RIGHT- LARRY O'BRIEN BROUGHT HIS SEVENTEEN SONS IN YESTERDAY TO GIT THEIR HAIRCUT-

GEO MCMANUS

AN' HOW COLD THE MORNIN'S WERE AN' HOW YOUR KID BROTHERS HATED SATURDAY NIGHT-

GIT THE ICE-PICK- THE WATER'S FROZEN-

WILL YOU TAKE YOUR FEET OUT OF THAT OVEN?

THE MINUTE YOUR MOTHER WENT OUT TO THE WOOD-SHED FER COAL AN' WOOD YOUR FATHER WOULD TOAST HIS FEET IN THE OVEN-

12 31

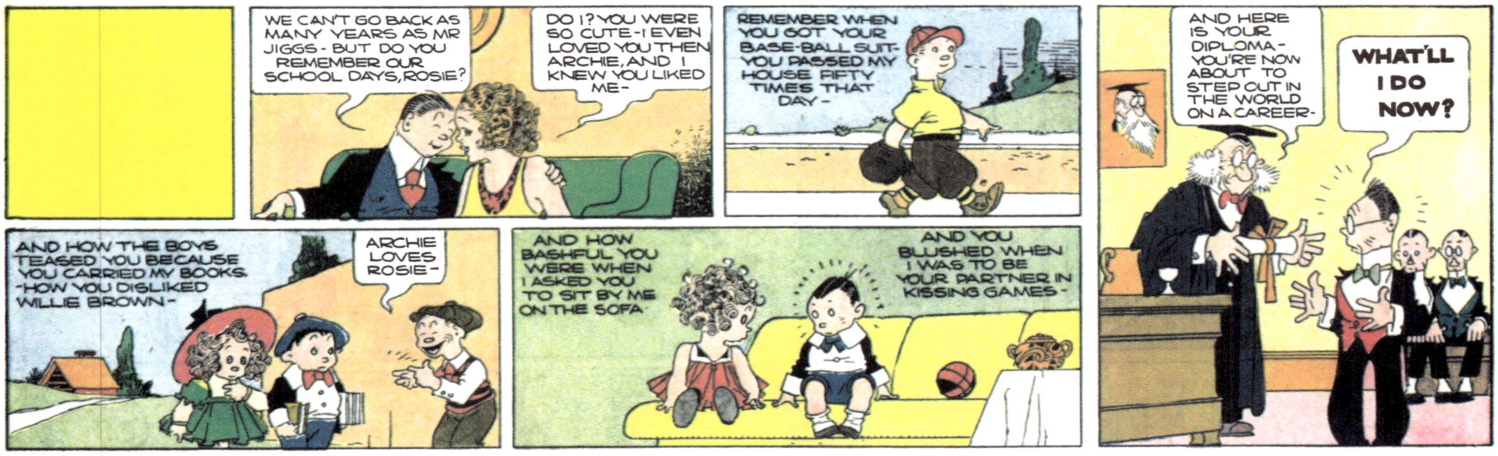

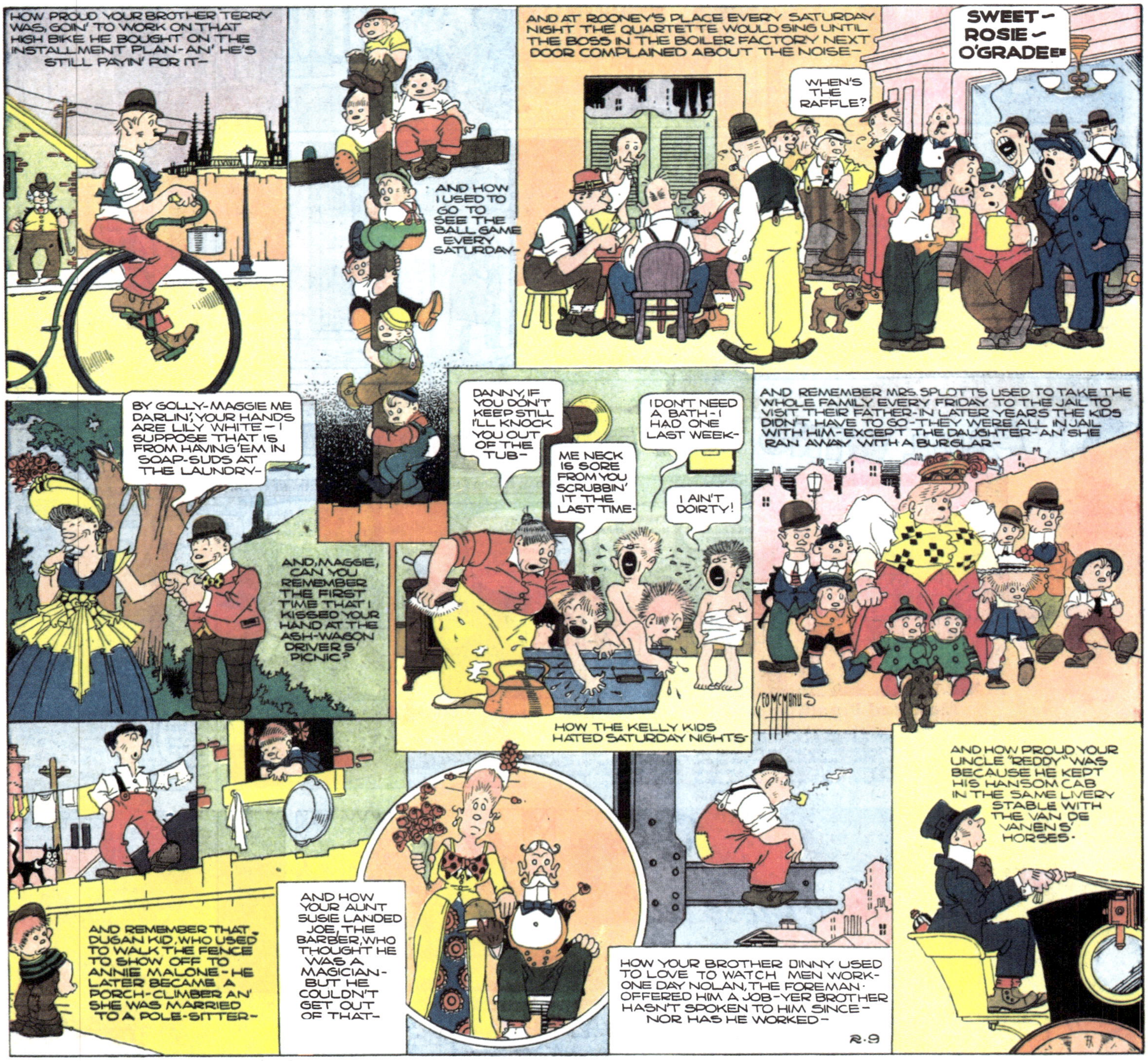

HOW PROUD YOUR BROTHER TERRY WAS, GOIN' TO WORK ON THAT HIGH BIKE HE BOUGHT ON THE INSTALLMENT PLAN - AN' HE'S STILL PAYIN' FOR IT -

AND HOW I USED TO GO TO SEE THE BALL GAME EVERY SATURDAY -

AND AT ROONEY'S PLACE EVERY SATURDAY NIGHT THE QUARTETTE WOULD SING UNTIL THE BOSS IN THE BOILER FACTORY NEXT DOOR COMPLAINED ABOUT THE NOISE -

SWEET - ROSIE - O'GRADEEE

WHEN'S THE RAFFLE?

BY GOLLY - MAGGIE ME DARLIN', YOUR HANDS ARE LILY WHITE - I SUPPOSE THAT IS FROM HAVING 'EM IN SOAP-SUDS AT THE LAUNDRY -

AND, MAGGIE, CAN YOU REMEMBER THE FIRST TIME THAT I KISSED YOUR HAND AT THE ASH-WAGON DRIVER'S PICNIC?

DANNY, IF YOU DON'T KEEP STILL I'LL KNOCK YOU OUT OF THE TUB -

ME NECK IS SORE FROM YOU SCRUBBIN' IT THE LAST TIME -

I DON'T NEED A BATH - I HAD ONE LAST WEEK -

I AIN'T DOIRTY!

HOW THE KELLY KIDS HATED SATURDAY NIGHTS -

AND REMEMBER MRS. SPLOTTS USED TO TAKE THE WHOLE FAMILY EVERY FRIDAY TO THE JAIL TO VISIT THEIR FATHER - IN LATER YEARS THE KIDS DIDN'T HAVE TO GO - THEY WERE ALL IN JAIL WITH HIM - EXCEPT THE DAUGHTER - AN' SHE RAN AWAY WITH A BURGLAR -

GEO McMANUS

AND REMEMBER THAT DUGAN KID, WHO USED TO WALK THE FENCE TO SHOW OFF TO ANNIE MALONE - HE LATER BECAME A PORCH-CLIMBER AN' SHE WAS MARRIED TO A POLE-SITTER -

AND HOW YOUR AUNT SUSIE LANDED JOE, THE BARBER, WHO THOUGHT HE WAS A MAGICIAN - BUT HE COULDN'T GET OUT OF THAT -

HOW YOUR BROTHER DINNY USED TO LOVE TO WATCH MEN WORK - ONE DAY NOLAN, THE FOREMAN OFFERED HIM A JOB - YER BROTHER HASN'T SPOKEN TO HIM SINCE - NOR HAS HE WORKED -

AND HOW PROUD YOUR UNCLE "REDDY" WAS BECAUSE HE KEPT HIS HANSOM CAB IN THE SAME LIVERY STABLE WITH THE VAN DE VANEN'S HORSES -

2-9

REMEMBER-MAGGIE-THE DAY YOUR SISTER WON THE DANCIN' CONTEST AT DINKY DEMON'S HALL? YOUR UNCLE AND TWO BROTHERS WERE THE JUDGES-

IS MARY DUGAN STILL GOING WITH THAT PLUMBER?

YOUR FATHER ALWAYS HAD TO ENTERTAIN YOUR SISTER'S BEAU- THE FOREMAN IN O'BRIEN'S COAL-YARD- WHILE SHE WAS BUSY TRYING TO GIT HER FEET IN HER SIZE TWO WHITE SHOES-

I'VE GOT A PITCHER IF YOU GOT A DIME AN' I'LL GO GET IT-

LET ME OFF AT DINTY'S-

AND HOW HAPPY WE'D BE IF WE GOT HOME AFTER A SUNDAY RIDE ON A STREET-CAR WITHOUT A BROKEN LEG- YOUR FATHER ALWAYS HAD A BROKEN BOTTLE ON HIS HIP-

AND HOW YOUR SISTER CRIED WHEN SHE WENT TO SEE THAT MELODRAMA, "HEARTS APART- OR WHERE IS THE ACE?" HER BEAU CRIED, TOO- FOR HIS MONEY BACK-

MY PROUD BEAUTY, I SHALL THROW YOU OFF YON CLIFF!

YOUR MOTHER USED TO SAVE ALL TH' OLD PAPERS AN' GIVE EM TO YOUR KID BROTHER TO SELL ON DARK CORNERS AT NIGHT AS EXTRAS-

I'M IN FAVOR OF THAT-

WUXTRA

REMEMBER WHEN YOUR COUSIN BERTHA LANDED THE TOWN BARBER AND HE GAVE HER A STOVE FOR A WEDDIN' PRESENT- ON THE FOURTH DAY OF THEIR HONEYMOON- SHE HIT HIM WITH IT-

WE'LL ALL MISS YOU AT THE LAUNDRY-

ARE THOSE HIS SHOES OR VIOLIN CASES?

I WONDER WHOSE SUIT HE BORROWED FOR THIS TIE-UP?

AND HOW THE GOSSIP FLEW WHEN MOLLY O'GALLON WAS SEEN WALKIN' PAST THE BRICK-YARD WITH POWDER ON HER FACE AN' RED CHEEKS-

AND AS A LITTLE KID YOU ALWAYS LOVED OUT-DOOR CONCERTS-

EIN- ZWIE- COMMENCE-

AND YOUR FAMILY SPENT ALL DAY SUNDAY TRYING TO GET YOUR FATHER TO PUT ON A SHIRT AND BY THE TIME HE DID- THE KIDS WERE SO DIRTY YOU COULDN'T GO OUT-

NO!

DO TELL-

AND SO I-

AND WHEN YOUR AUNT BESSIE WENT TO THE BEACH NO ONE COULD SEE TH' OCEAN- AN' YOUR UNCLE ALWAYS FELT AT HOME IN A STRIPED BATHING-SUIT- HE WAS USED TO STRIPES-

8-16

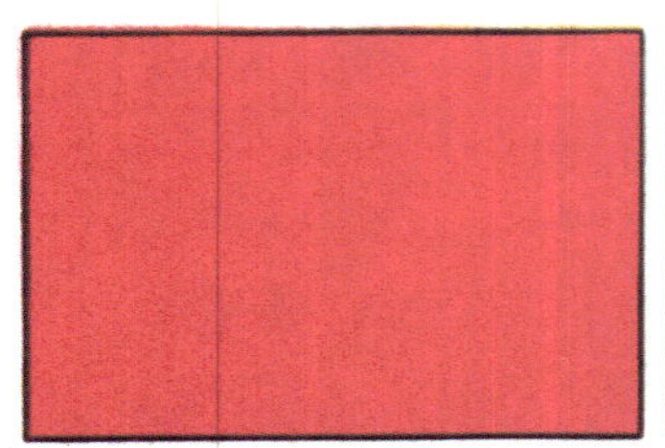

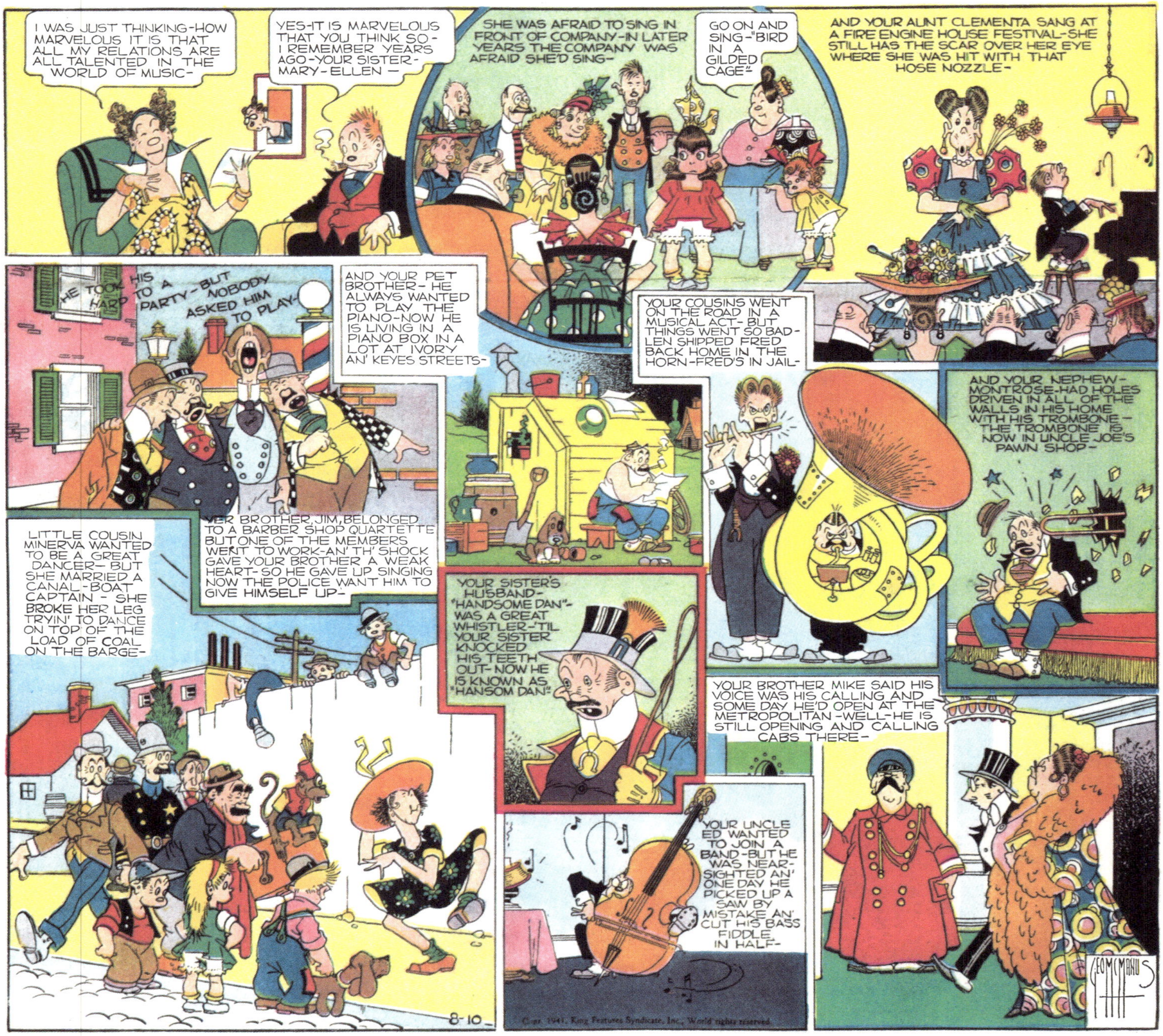

I WAS JUST THINKING-HOW MARVELOUS IT IS THAT ALL MY RELATIONS ARE ALL TALENTED IN THE WORLD OF MUSIC-

YES-IT IS MARVELOUS THAT YOU THINK SO-I REMEMBER YEARS AGO-YOUR SISTER-MARY-ELLEN-

SHE WAS AFRAID TO SING IN FRONT OF COMPANY-IN LATER YEARS THE COMPANY WAS AFRAID SHE'D SING-

GO ON AND SING-"BIRD IN A GILDED CAGE"

AND YOUR AUNT CLEMENTA SANG AT A FIRE ENGINE HOUSE FESTIVAL-SHE STILL HAS THE SCAR OVER HER EYE WHERE SHE WAS HIT WITH THAT HOSE NOZZLE-

HE TOOK HIS HARP TO A PARTY-BUT NOBODY ASKED HIM TO PLAY-

AND YOUR PET BROTHER-HE ALWAYS WANTED TO PLAY THE PIANO-NOW HE IS LIVING IN A PIANO BOX IN A LOT AT IVORY AN' KEYES STREETS-

YOUR COUSINS WENT ON THE ROAD IN A MUSICAL ACT-BUT THINGS WENT SO BAD-LEN SHIPPED FRED BACK HOME IN THE HORN-FRED'S IN JAIL-

AND YOUR NEPHEW-MONTROSE-HAD HOLES DRIVEN IN ALL OF THE WALLS IN HIS HOME WITH HIS TROMBONE-THE TROMBONE IS NOW IN UNCLE JOE'S PAWN SHOP-

LITTLE COUSIN MINERVA WANTED TO BE A GREAT DANCER-BUT SHE MARRIED A CANAL-BOAT CAPTAIN-SHE BROKE HER LEG TRYIN' TO DANCE ON TOP OF THE LOAD OF COAL ON THE BARGE-

YER BROTHER, JIM, BELONGED TO A BARBER SHOP QUARTETTE BUT ONE OF THE MEMBERS WENT TO WORK-AN' TH' SHOCK GAVE YOUR BROTHER A WEAK HEART-SO HE GAVE UP SINGING NOW THE POLICE WANT HIM TO GIVE HIMSELF UP-

YOUR SISTER'S HUSBAND-"HANDSOME DAN"-WAS A GREAT WHISTLER-'TIL YOUR SISTER KNOCKED HIS TEETH OUT-NOW HE IS KNOWN AS "HANSOM DAN"

YOUR BROTHER MIKE SAID HIS VOICE WAS HIS CALLING AND SOME DAY HE'D OPEN AT THE METROPOLITAN-WELL-HE IS STILL OPENING AND CALLING CABS THERE-

YOUR UNCLE ED WANTED TO JOIN A BAND-BUT HE WAS NEAR-SIGHTED AN' ONE DAY HE PICKED UP A SAW BY MISTAKE AN' CUT HIS BASS FIDDLE IN HALF-

8-10

Copr. 1941, King Features Syndicate, Inc., World rights reserved.

GEO MCMANUS

GRACIOUS! WHERE IS ARCHIE? I JUST STEPPED OUT OF THE ROOM TO MAKE HIM A CUP OF TEA - NOW HE'S GONE -
HE RAN OUT THE FRONT DOOR - HE WAS MUMBLIN' TO HIMSELF - HE SEEMED TO BE ANGRY ABOUT SOMETHING - HE MUST BE AT HIS OFFICE BY NOW -
I'LL CALL HIM UP - I CAN'T UNDERSTAND WHAT CAME OVER HIM - HELLO!
OH - YOU OUGHT TO KNOW WHY I AM ANGRY - DON'T THINK I AM JEALOUS - BUT I SAW THAT PICTURE OF A SOLDIER ON YOUR PIANO - I CAN'T SAY I ADMIRE YOUR CHOICE - AS HE CERTAINLY DOESN'T LOOK INTELLIGENT -
WHY - ARCHIE - YOU SILLY BOY - WHAT ARE YOU TALKING ABOUT? THAT'S A VERY HANDSOME BOY THAT I'M IN LOVE WITH -
ULP!
IT'S YOU - DON'T YOU REMEMBER -? IT WAS TAKEN TWO YEARS AGO AT A MASQUERADE BALL -
11-30
Copr. 1941, King Features Syndicate, Inc., World rights reserved.
DADDY - YOU LOOK AS IF YOUR THOUGHTS WERE MILES AWAY -
I'M JUST THINKIN' YEARS BACK - DAUGHTER - I KIN SEE YOU NOW - JUST A LITTLE LASS - STANDING IN THE BACK YARD WAITING FOR YOUR UNCLE TO COME HOME SATURDAY NIGHT —
THERE HE IS - I WONDER IF HE BROUGHT ME PRETZELS?
THAT CAN'T BE HIM - HE'S WALKING STRAIGHT -
AND WHEN AUNT MIN WENT OUT RIDING WITH THE TOWN'S DOG-CATCHER -
FIRST - THE RIG BROKE DOWN - THEN THE HORSE -
AND MAGGIE ALWAYS THOUGHT YOUR UNCLE BIMMY HAD TAKIN' WAYS - AND AN EYE FER BEAUTY - HE WAS ONLY ON THE FORCE TWO MONTHS - AND ARRESTED EVERYONE IN HIS FAMILY - AND ANOTHER POLICEMAN PINCHED HIM -
AND THOSE GRAND EVENINGS AT DINTY'S - NEVER A DULL MOMENT - THERE WERE NO 'PHONES IN THEM DAYS - YOUR WIFE WOULD COME AND GET YOU - - YOUR GRANDFATHER WALKED TO DINTY'S EVERY NIGHT - AND WUZ CARRIED HOME - NO ONE EVER WON AN ARGUMENT - THEY ALWAYS ENDED UP IN A FIGHT - AND NO ONE EVER WON ANY OF THEM -
I'LL NEVER FORGIT THE DAY SOMEONE IN THE FAMILY BROKE GRANDPA'S FINE MUSTACHE COFFEE CUP - HE HOLLERED UNTIL HE FAINTED - THEN SOMEONE GAVE HIM A CUP OF WATER AN' HE PASSED OUT COMPLETELY -
AND HOW STUCK UP THE SEYMOUR ORLESS FAMILY WAS WHEN HE WON THAT BIKE AT THE SLAUGHTER HOUSE TURKEY RAFFLE -
I HAD BETTER RING THE BELL - I SEE A HORSE -
DON'T FAIL TO PASS THE JIGGS' SHANTY - I HOPE THEY SEE US PASS -
POP - WHEN CAN I BORROW THIS BIKE TO TAKE ME GIRL OUT?
AND COUSIN JOE USED TO SHAVE IN THE KITCHEN - SINK ON SUNDAY MORNIN' - THE BREAKFAST ALWAYS TASTED LIKE SOAP -
AT LEAST TWICE A DAY - SOME ONE ROCKED ON TABBY'S TAIL - AND EVERYBODY HAD SCARS ON THEIR SHINS FROM THE ROCKERS —
YE-OW!
EVERY KID IN THE NEIGHBORHOOD HATED SATURDAY NIGHT - - EVEN THE MEN HATED WATER - WHEN IT WUZ IN A GLASS —
Copr. 1941, King Features Syndicate, Inc., World rights reserved.
WE NEVER KNEW WHERE THE BARBER THAT MARYELLEN MARRIED CAME FROM - AND AFTER THEY WERE MARRIED SIX MONTHS - NO ONE KNEW WHERE HE WENT -
AIN'T LOVE GRAND?
LOOKIT THAT - MISS TADAY HAS RED POWDER ON HER FACE -
SHE GITS IT FROM THE BRICK-YARD WHERE HER FATHER WORKS -
EVERY SUNDAY WE SAT ON THE STEPS AN' WATCHED THE PARADE - THE ODOR OF CAMPHOR FILLED THE AIR - -
11-30

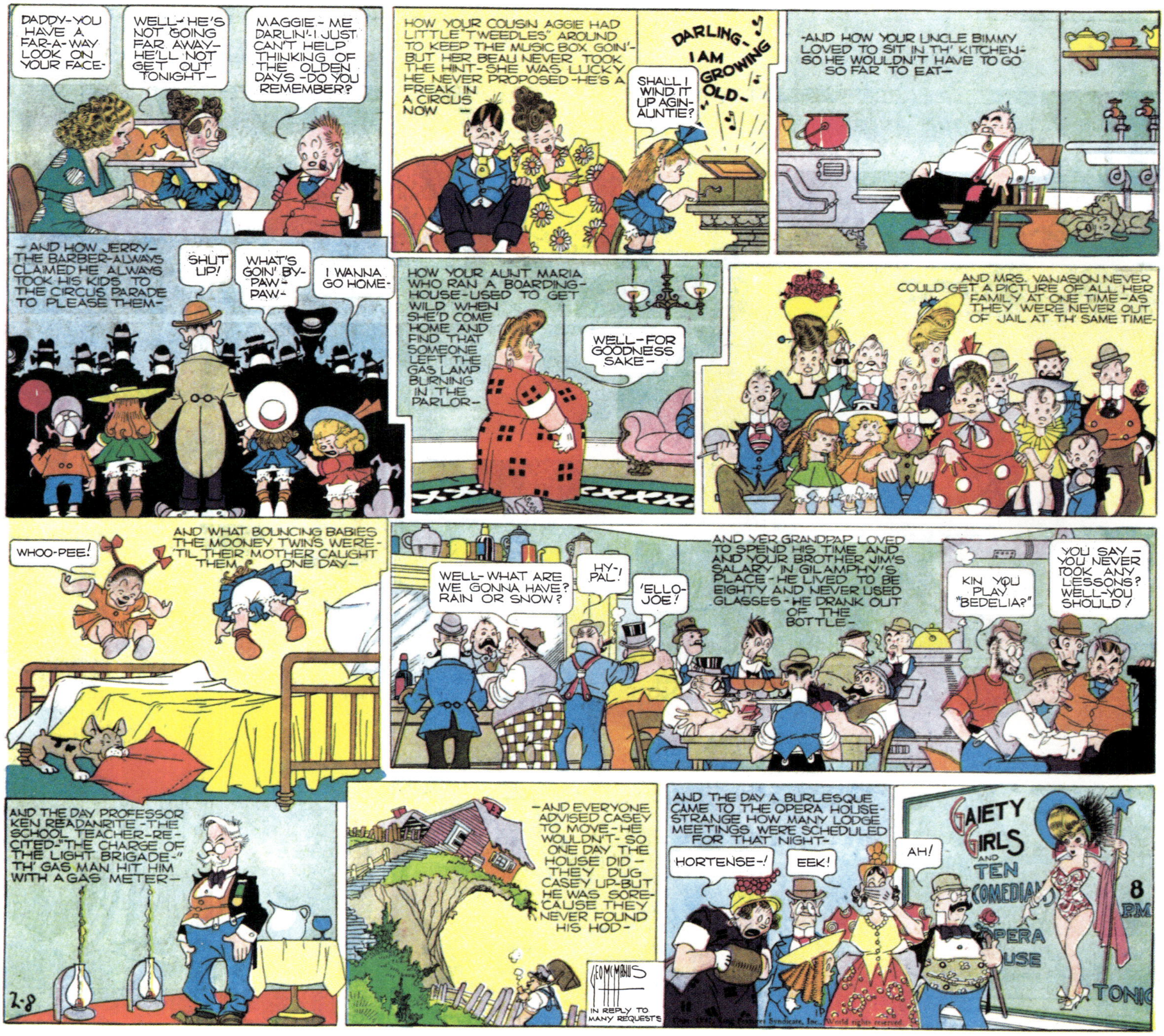

DADDY-YOU HAVE A FAR-A-WAY LOOK ON YOUR FACE-
WELL-HE'S NOT GOING FAR AWAY-HE'LL NOT GET OUT TONIGHT-
MAGGIE-ME DARLIN'-I JUST CAN'T HELP THINKING OF THE OLDEN DAYS-DO YOU REMEMBER?

HOW YOUR COUSIN AGGIE HAD LITTLE "TWEEDLES" AROUND TO KEEP THE MUSIC BOX GOIN'-BUT HER BEAU NEVER TOOK THE HINT-SHE WAS LUCKY HE NEVER PROPOSED-HE'S A FREAK IN A CIRCUS NOW-
DARLING-I AM GROWING OLD-
SHALL I WIND IT UP AGIN-AUNTIE?

-AND HOW YOUR UNCLE BIMMY LOVED TO SIT IN TH' KITCHEN-SO HE WOULDN'T HAVE TO GO SO FAR TO EAT-

-AND HOW JERRY-THE BARBER-ALWAYS CLAIMED HE ALWAYS TOOK HIS KIDS TO THE CIRCUS PARADE TO PLEASE THEM-
SHUT UP!
WHAT'S GOIN' BY-PAW-PAW-
I WANNA GO HOME-

HOW YOUR AUNT MARIA WHO RAN A BOARDING-HOUSE-USED TO GET WILD WHEN SHE'D COME HOME AND FIND THAT SOMEONE LEFT THE GAS LAMP BURNING IN THE PARLOR-
WELL-FOR GOODNESS SAKE-

AND MRS. VANASION NEVER COULD GET A PICTURE OF ALL HER FAMILY AT ONE TIME-AS THEY WERE NEVER OUT OF JAIL AT TH' SAME TIME-

WHOO-PEE!
AND WHAT BOUNCING BABIES THE MOONEY TWINS WERE-'TIL THEIR MOTHER CAUGHT THEM ONE DAY-

AND YER GRANDPAP LOVED TO SPEND HIS TIME AND AND YOUR BROTHER JIM'S SALARY IN GILAMPHY'S PLACE-HE LIVED TO BE EIGHTY AND NEVER USED GLASSES-HE DRANK OUT OF THE BOTTLE-
WELL-WHAT ARE WE GONNA HAVE? RAIN OR SNOW?
HY-PAL!
'ELLO-JOE!
KIN YOU PLAY "BEDELIA?"
YOU SAY-YOU NEVER TOOK ANY LESSONS? WELL-YOU SHOULD!

AND THE DAY PROFESSOR KEN READANRITE-THE SCHOOL TEACHER-RECITED-"THE CHARGE OF THE LIGHT BRIGADE-" TH' GAS MAN HIT HIM WITH A GAS METER-
2-8

-AND EVERYONE ADVISED CASEY TO MOVE-HE WOULDN'T-SO ONE DAY THE HOUSE DID-THEY DUG CASEY UP-BUT HE WAS SORE-CAUSE THEY NEVER FOUND HIS HOD-
GEO McMANUS
IN REPLY TO MANY REQUESTS

AND THE DAY A BURLESQUE CAME TO THE OPERA HOUSE-STRANGE HOW MANY LODGE MEETINGS WERE SCHEDULED FOR THAT NIGHT-
HORTENSE-!
EEK!
AH!
GAIETY GIRLS AND TEN COMEDIANS
OPERA HOUSE
8 PM
TONIG

MARY-HOW DO I LOOK IN MY MASQUERADE COSTUME FOR THE BIG BALL TONIGHT- I'M ANXIOUS TO SEE WHAT KIND OF A COSTUME ARCHIE WILL WEAR-
YOU LOOK GORGEOUS-ROSIE-
GOSH-I FEEL LIKE A REAL SOLDIER IN THIS COSTUME- I WONDER WHAT ROSIE IS GOING TO WEAR?
?
HEY-WHAT'S THE IDEA OF YOU BEIN' AWAY FROM YER' BARRACKS AT THIS HOUR?
COME ALONG-
MP
MP
STEP LIVELY-
BUT LISTEN-I'M NOT A REAL SOLDIER-I AM JUST WEARING THIS OUTFIT-
OH-A SPY-WELL-
SAY-CAN I PHONE ROSIE-
SHUT UP!
Copr. 1942, King Features Syndicate, Inc., World rights reserved
4-26
MAGGIE-REMEMBER THE OLD DAYS WHEN YOUR UNCLE TIM USED TO SIT ON THE HORSE TROUGH AND RAVE ABOUT WHAT HIS FATHER DID IN TH' CIVIL WAR-
DIDN'T ANY BODY HELP YOUR DAD IN THE WAR?
DID THE GENERALS ALWAYS CONSULT HIM FIRST?
YOUR COUSIN "BOBO" AS A BABY HAD A BIG HEAD-AN' EVERYONE THOUGHT HE'D BE A BIG SHOT-HE STILL HAS THE BIG HEAD-AN' LOTS OF FOLKS WISH HE WAS SHOT-
AND THOSE PICNICS-MRS. MUNIGAN'S FAMILY WOULD COME HOME ALL IN-HER HUSBAND WAS ALL IN TOO SO THEY USED TO LEAVE HIM IN THE PARK- HE'D SPEND HOURS TRYIN' TO FEED AN IRON DEER-
MAMA-WHAT'S THE MATTER WITH PAPA? I SAW HIM DRINKING WATER?
I KNEW THAT THEIR MARRIAGE WOULDN'T LAST- SHE MADE HIM GO OUT AND LOOK FOR WORK-AN' HE NEVER DID COME BACK-
AN' NOW HER DAD HASN'T ANYONE TO LOAF WITH HIM-
-AND UNCLE "SITTEN BILL" USED TO MAKE THE KIDS LISTEN TO HIM TELL BED TIME STORIES SO THEY'D GET SLEEPY-THEY NEVER GOT SLEEPY-BUT THEY WENT TO BED ANYWAY-AND HIS WIFE WOULD RATHER CARRY COAL THAN LISTEN-
WHO ARE THOSE TWO WOMEN HE IS DANCING WITH?
SHE MUST TRAVEL AS FREIGHT-
THE GOOD OLD DAYS OF VAUDEVILLE-TOMMY AN' HIS SISTER DID A DANCING ACT-HE USED TO SWING HER AROUND IN THE AIR-BY THE WAY-WHERE IS HE BURIED?
"AND WHEN THE CATS USED TO GET ON THE FENCE IN THE BACK YARD-
AND "BUTCH" HAD TO TAKE THE KIDS TO WORK WITH HIM SO HE WOULD BE SURE TO GET HOME WITH HIS SALARY-HE LET AGNES CARRY HIS SHOVEL-HE'D LET HER CARRY HIM IF HE THOUGHT SHE COULD-
AND THE TIME ALDERMAN HENNEHAN GAVE A PARTY ON TOP OF MIKE DUGAN'S TENEMENT HOUSE TO GIT VOTES-HE GOT TWO-AND MIGHT HAVE GOTTEN THREE BUT HIS OTHER BROTHER COULDN'T GIT OUT TO VOTE-I NEVER SAW SO MANY PATROL WAGONS AT A PARTY IN MY LIFE-
YOUR UNCLE "DINNY" WORKED IN A LUMBER YARD-HE USED TO PICK UP WHAT HE CALLED "SPLINTERS" AND BRING THEM HOME FOR THE FIRE-THEY NOW LIVE IN THE FINEST FRAME HOUSE ON THE BLOCK-
4-26
AND POOR OLD "RAINBOW-NOSE" RYANGIN USED TO GIT UP EVERY MORNING AND CRACK THE ICE IN THE WATER PITCHER SO THE KIDS COULD WASH TO GO TO SCHOOL-THEY WERE ALWAYS HAPPY WHEN IT WAS FROZEN SOLID-BUT SATURDAY WAS SAD FOR THE KIDS-THEY HAD HOT WATER FOR THE WASH-TUB-
GEO McMANUS

GOSH - I CAN'T GET ROSIE OFF MY MIND!
LISTEN - DON'T BE A SAP - IF SHE WON'T TALK TO YOU WHEN YOU CALL HER UP - JUST FORGET HER - BE A MAN -
I GUESS YOU'RE RIGHT! A MAN IS A FOOL FOR WORRYING ABOUT ANY GIRL -
YOU SAID IT - I'M GLAD YOU ARE COMING AROUND TO MY WAY OF THINKING -
I FEEL BETTER AFTER TALKIN' TO HIM - ROSIE CAN'T MAKE A FOOL OF ME -
I'LL NOT CALL HER UP AGAIN -
BUT - I'LL JUST PASS HER HOUSE ON MY WAY HOME -
HUH - I WONDER IF SHE'S GOING OUT WITH SOME OTHER GUY?
8-9
Copr. 1942, King Features Syndicate, Inc., World rights reserved
ISN'T THIS WAR AWFUL? JUST THINK OF THE INCONVENIENCE WE'RE PUT TO -
ISN'T IT AWFUL?
WHAT ARE YOUSE TALKIN' ABOUT? WHY - IN THE OLD DAYS - ALL WE HAD WUZ -
ONE OLD COAL-OIL LAMP FER ALL OF US TO READ BY - AND THE LAMP WAS PERFUME COMPARED TO GRANDPAW'S PIPE -
STUFF YOUR COAT IN THAT BROKEN WINDOW PANE - TH' SNOW IS BLOWING IN AGAIN -
HERO HARRY
AN' THOUGHT NOTHIN' OF WALKIN' SIX MILES TO SCHOOL EVERY MORNING - AN' THOUGHT VERY LITTLE OF OUR TEACHER -
IF I AM PROMOTED TODAY - I WILL BE IN TH' SAME CLASS AS MY PAW -
RING YOUR BELL - JOHN I SEE A HORSE
AN' YOU DON'T HAVE TO LOOK AT SIGHTS LIKE THIS - AS WE DID -
AN' WHEN YOU VISITED - YOU HAD TO SIT IN THE PARLOR AND SPEND HOURS LYING HOW TALENTED LITTLE MARY-ELLEN WAS -
ISN'T SHE LIGHT ON HER FEET?
AND IN TH' HEAD - TOO.!!
AN' YER FATHER WOULD GIVE YOU A NICE RED-HANDLED HATCHET ON CHRISTMAS - THEN TELL YOU TO GO OUT IN TH' YARD AND PLAY -
WE WERE GLAD IF WE COULD EVEN GET ON A STREET CAR - LET ALONE RIDE IN AN AUTO -
AND FOR FIVE TO SLEEP IN ONE BED WASN'T ANYTHING - THIRTEEN WAS CONSIDERED UNLUCKY - THEN WAKE UP IN THE MORNING AND HAVE TO LOOK AT THOSE PICTURES OF GRANDPAW AND GRANDMAW -
AN' EVERY KID IN TH' BLOCK HAD BLISTERS ON THEIR HANDS FROM GITTING TH' FEMALES OF THE FAMILY IN SHAPE -
HEAVE!!
WE NEVER KNEW WHAT IT WAS TO BE WARM -
WE HAD A GRATE FIREPLACE IN EACH ROOM AND IT WOULD BE GREAT - IF THERE WAS A FIRE IN THE GRATE -
WELCOME
8-9
AND THE EVENINGS I SPENT STARVING TO DEATH AT THOSE BANQUETS -
UNACCUSTOMED AS I AM TO PUBLIC - SPEAKING -
I HOPE HE WON'T RECITE "GUNGA-DIN" AGAIN -
NO USE HOPING - HE WILL -
ALL THE KIDS IN THE NEIGHBORHOOD WERE AFRAID OF TH' COPS - AND TH' COPS WERE AFRAID OF EVERY - BODY IN THE NEIGHBORHOOD -
GEO McMANUS
Copr. 1942, King Features Syndicate, Inc., World rights reserved

DA-DA-
QUIET-DOVEY! HERE COME THOSE PESTS-MR. AND MRS. DISSENDAT !!

THERE GOES THE DOORBELL — JUST LET THEM RING UNTIL THEY GET TIRED - WE WON'T ANSWER !!
GOO !!
SH-SH-H- THEY'RE STILL THERE !!

KENESAW - I SAID - RING IT AGAIN -
YES- MY DEAR !!

?
Copr. 1945, King Features Syndicate, Inc.

WA-A
World rights reserved.
12-23

WE WERE BEGINNING TO BELIEVE YOU WERE OUT WHEN WE HEARD, THE LITTLE DARLINGS VOICE !!
OH-WHY-YES-I-OH-I MEAN WE WERE JUST THINKING OF YOU-- WE'RE SO GLAD TO SEE YOU !!
GOO!
GEO MCMANUS

JUST THINK !! IT'S OUR THIRTY-THIRD ANNIVERSARY-HOW THINGS HAVE CHANGED - WHEN I THINK BACK !!
YEP! REMEMBER WHEN WE LIVED IN THE SHANTY UP ON DUGAN'S BLUFF-AN' YOU INVITED YOUR RELATIVES TO VISIT US !!!

THE SHANTY SLID OFF THE BLUFF- YER UNCLE WAS SORE- BECAUSE HE NEVER FOUND HIS PICK AND SHOVEL AGAIN!

-AND THE DAY WE RENTED A RIG-AND WHEN WE PASSED A GLUE FACTORY- THE HORSE RAN AWAY !!!

AND YOUR UNCLE BEN WAS ALWAYS AT THE FREE LUNCH COUNTER-IT WAS EASY TO TELL IF HE HAD BEEN IN- IF ALL THE FISH BALLS WERE GONE HE HAD BEEN THERE AND GONE !!!

AND SWEET SATURDAY NIGHT WHEN THE FAMILY WOULD GATHER ON TH' FRONT STOOP AND LATER IT TOOK THE COPS TO SEPARATE 'EM !!!

AND WHEN YOUR GRANDFATHER CALLED-WE ALL HAD TO LISTEN TO WHAT HE DID IN THE CIVIL WAR- IT WAS ALWAYS INTERESTING-AS HE NEVER TOLD IT ALIKE TWICE-

-AND YOUR BROTHER DINNY INSISTED ON THE COPS TAKING HIM PAST HIS HOUSE SO HE COULD WAVE TO HIS KIDS TO LET 'EM KNOW HE WOULDN'T BE HOME FOR DINNER !!!
PATROL

HERMAN-THE BARBER-WHO COURTED AUNT SUSIE-WANTED TO BE AN ORGANIST- IN THEM DAYS-LITTLE ROSE-MARY WAS SOMEWHAT OF A CRITIC---

AN' NONE OF US KIDS MISSED THE BIG LEAGUE BALL GAMES UNTIL THEY BUILT A BRICK WALL AROUND THE PARK !!!
GEO MCMANUS
Copr. 1945, King Features Syndicate, Inc., World rights reserved.
12-23

IT'S SO LOVELY HERE AT HOME-I CANNOT UNDERSTAND WHY YOU WANT TO GO OUT-
BUT, MOTHER-YOU MUSTN'T FORGET-DADDY IS A BUSINESS-MAN AND MUST GO TO WORK-
YES-I HAVE A DIRECTOR'S MEETIN' TODAY-I'M LATE NOW-ME DARLIN'-
HOW'D YOU BURN YER HANDS-TOM?
ME WIFE THREW A HOT STOVE AT ME AN' I TRIED TO CATCH IT-
HOW'D YOU PAY YOUR RENT THIS MONTH?
I SOLD TH' KITCHEN DOOR-
HERBIE-YER MOTHER TOLD ME TO FIND YOU AN' TELL YOU TO GO FIND YER FATHER-
DANNY-STOP THROWIN' ROCKS AT YER BROTHER-THROW 'EM AT YOUR FATHER-
IS IT TRUE-YER HUSBAND IS THINKIN' ABOUT GOIN' TO WORK?
WHO SAID HE COULD THINK?
JOHNNIE-STOP KICKIN' WILLIE-SLAP HIM-
GIT A DIME'S WORTH AND TELL DUGAN NOT SO MUCH FOAM-
DOT ANY CHEWIN'-GUM-BINNIE?
ARF-
WHEN I GIT THROUGH WITH YOU-YOU WILL KNOW IT-
DON'T TALK-FIGHT-
SAMMY-DON'T MOVE-LET THE AUTO DRIVE AROUND YOU-
BEE-DA LUM-BO-
HELLO-TESSIE-
I'M GONNA PUNCH Y' IN THE NOSE-MICKEY-
HOW'M I DOIN', KID?
WIL-LEE-
ONLY A BIRD IN A GILDED CAGE
YEA-TH' PAINT COMES OFF-
IT'S GRAND TO SEE TH' OLD NEIGHBORHOOD AGIN'-
HEY-CHARLIE-JERRY'S GOT TH' MUMPS-
HELLO, MRS KATZENRATS-WHEN DID YER HUSBAND GIT OUT OF JAIL?
WAKE UP, MIKE-YOU HAVE BEEN ASLEEP FOR DAYS-
I'LL BE SEEIN' YOU-
YES-BUT IT HAS CHANGED-IT'S QUIET NOW-
LET'S SEE YOU FALL ON YER HEAD-
LOOKIT-
ARF-
SAY "UNCLE"
SOCK HIM-

A NOTE *from the Publisher*

The original art for this book has long been scattered to the winds. Employing laser-scan color separation technology, *Jiggs Is Back* has been reproduced from the original Sunday newsprint funny papers as they first appeared—in some instances more than sixty years ago. Although reduced in size, the tone, color pattern, and quality of each of these reproductions remains faithful to the age of their ultimate origin. "The miracle of modern technology," et cetera.

MAGGIE REMEMBER-WHEN WE WERE "KIDS" YOU HAD A DOG NAMED "FIFI" AND I HAD A MUTT NAMED "FLEA FLEA"-

AND WAS YOUR UNCLE SORE THE DAY HE WAS IN A DEPARTMENT STORE WHEN THE LIGHTS WENT OUT-HE WAS IN THE PIANO DEPARTMENT- JERRY THE BARBER WAS IN THE JEWELRY DEPARTMENT-

REMEMBER YOUR LITTLE BROTHER "TIMMY" WAS THE ONLY ONE IN THE CLASS ONE DAY THAT COULD ANSWER THE TEACHER'S QUESTION?
-- SHE WANTED TO KNOW WHO HIT HER IN THE EYE WITH A PIECE OF CHALK

AND YOUR UNCLE "RUSTY" ALWAYS FELT AT HOME IN A PATROL WAGON-
HY- ED-
OLICE PATROL

REMEMBER WHEN THE BOYS WOULD GO ON A FISHING TRIP TO GET AWAY FROM THE CONGESTION IN THE CITY-